**SONS
OF THE
DARK**

escape

Also in the
SONS OF THE DARK
series

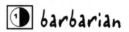 barbarian

SONS
OF THE
DARK

escape

LYNNE EWING

HYPERION/NEW YORK

First Edition
1 3 5 7 9 10 8 6 4 2
Printed in the United States of America

Library of Congress Cataloging-in-Publication Data on file.
ISBN 0-7868-1812-3

Visit www.volobooks.com

For Vanessa and Noel,
bad boy experts

A.D. 1768

Samuel stopped running and, without the crashing sound of his own footsteps, he became aware of the deep stillness pressing around him; even the birds had ceased singing. He slipped between two maples and waited for Macduff to catch up to him. The last time they had been separated, Samuel had called his friend's name. This time fear silenced him. He didn't understand his growing apprehension, but he had a strange feeling that if he did yell, he'd awaken something malevolent and better left asleep.

Behind him in the sycamore hollow, leaves rippled on the low-hanging branches, even though no wind stirred the air. Every instinct told him to flee but instead he started back down the hill, his mouth dry and filled with the bitter taste of alarm. Maybe Macduff had fallen and needed his help.

They never should have ventured into these woods. He knew that now, but a frontiersman at the fort had promised to give Samuel an elixir to cure his great-grandfather's cough, and he had been determined to get the medicine. But Macduff had had misgivings from the start, because explorers said the forest was haunted. Samuel had finally convinced Macduff that the ghost stories were only tales the Shawnee told to keep pioneers from settling on the sacred hunting grounds of Can-tuck-ee. Now he wasn't sure.

When he reached the bottom of the hill, he took one slow, exploratory step forward and grabbed a swaying branch. "Macduff?"

Macduff spun around, startled, and clutched Samuel's arm.

"There," Macduff whispered anxiously, and pointed to a mysterious shadow unfurling in the gloomy shade.

A phantom formed from the darkness, its fierce amber eyes staring back at them with deadly hunger.

Then the creature let out a low, snuffling laugh, and its hot breath filled the forest with carrion stench.

Macduff turned sharply and broke into a run. Samuel sprinted after him, knowing it was the wrong thing to do; fleeing from a predator only triggered its instinct to chase. And this was no ordinary beast; it was man-size and ran on two feet. It burst through the underbrush, chasing after them at incredible speed. Branches snapped and, overhead, fiery sunlight flashed between the leaves, blinding Samuel. He leaped over a log and slammed into the trapper from the fort.

Samuel was relieved they'd found help. Macduff tried to warn the trapper they were being chased. But the trapper just chuckled with the same snuffling laugh as the creature and brought the barrel of his rifle down on Macduff's chest, knocking him backward. Samuel tried to pull Macduff away.

"I guess I caught myself two strong lads to sell to the devil." The trapper's voice boomed, startling birds into flight, and then he brought the rifle down again.

A paralyzing blow cracked Samuel's skull, and he fell to the ground, captured.

CHAPTER ONE

HEN NIGHT HAD settled and silence covered the roughly built shacks, Samuel slipped from the hut he had shared with Macduff. Cool, slick mud squeezed between his toes and a chill rose up through his bones. Torch flames cast an orange light over the rows of thatched huts and made shadows shudder and jump around him. But the fires did little to warm the air, and instead of rising, the smoke fell to the ground and curled around his ankles, then rose sinuously back up his bare legs and chest. Another time, the fumes might have stopped him, but on this night he was determined.

5

Everyone said escape was impossible, but, in spite of the warnings, Macduff had run. No one had seen him since. Samuel had planned to go with him, but at the last minute the master had taken Samuel hunting for wild boar. He didn't know if Macduff had gotten away, or if guards had captured him, but if there was any chance to break free from this nightmare, Samuel was going to try.

Each day, he descended into the dust-choked pits with hundreds of drugged and defeated *servi*: youths who had been kidnapped from the earth realm and imprisoned in Nefandus. He wasn't sure how long he had been there—months maybe, or even a year or more. His hands were scarred now, the palms coarsened with calluses from working with a shovel and pick, but his rebellious nature had never left him. Even the master's beatings hadn't tamed his heart. He had thick scars on his back, where the whip had shredded his skin, and his ribs still ached from his last flogging.

Like most *servi*, he could transform into shadow and glide through the night, a phantom shade, but racing through darkness would have aroused more suspicion than if he had been found wandering aimlessly about the run-down shacks. He squeezed behind the shelters and scrambled over a stone wall into the waste yard where injured *servi* were abandoned. The Master discarded the wounded and no longer fed them, but because he had also made them immortal, they couldn't die and escape their suffering.

Desperate eyes stared up at him. They sat hunched together on sagging wood floors beneath frayed burlap roofs. Some were too ill to crawl to shelter, and so they lay in the swampy mud, flies clustering thickly over their bare necks and hair.

Samuel lifted a bone-thin boy onto a soiled straw mat, and as he did, countless skeletal hands reached for him. Whispers rose in a haunting chorus, pleading for his help. Reluctantly, he stepped around them. He couldn't take care of that many and still escape.

Samuel had spent many nights hunting rodents in the compound to feed the castoffs, and now guilt overwhelmed him, leaving his chest hollow. Who would care for them once he was gone?

Suddenly the air pulsed with buzzing energy. A flurry of blue sparks swept around him and settled on his shoulders, the embers squirming across his flesh. Behind him, the moaning stopped and even the most crippled tried to drag themselves to the side of the path. The unpleasant vibration meant that the guards called Regulators were near.

Frantic, Samuel backed away, his fingers tracing over the rough stone wall, searching for a cranny in which to hide, but before he could find one, two Regulators turned the corner. Their black boots sloshed through the mud, as if they were unaware of the kids in their way. The taller one turned his bearish head and glared at Samuel, his eyes rheumy and yellow.

Samuel bowed to show respect and tried to control his breathing. He hoped they couldn't sense he was no longer medicated. He had seen what happened to *servi* who refused to drink the hana berry juice. Macduff had told him to stop taking his daily ration, because the beverage wasn't for their health, as the master had said, but it was rather a potion to keep them drugged and easily controlled. Samuel edged away, imitating the shuffling gait of a *servus*, but his heart hammered so loudly he felt certain they could hear it.

The first time he had seen Regulators he had been terrified. Since then he had become accustomed to their appearance and odor. He wondered what made strong young men and women volunteer to be sentinels to the primal force that ruled Nefandus, knowing its evil would eventually infect them and distort their bodies until they became monstrous imitations of what they had once been. The two marching past him now were muscular and big-boned, newly recruited; their faces had only begun to change, and their brawny bodies weren't misshapen yet.

The scent of heated iron made Samuel stop. He had sidled down the wall without watching where he was going, and now two men holding glowing red branding irons walked toward him. He swallowed hard to keep the bile from rising and wondered again what they had used for heat. Magic ignited the fires in Nefandus, and the flames burned cold.

Screams soon echoed into the night. The shrill cries came from new arrivals who were being branded. The lowest ones, destined to be workers in the pit, received the trident. The odor of burning flesh mingled with the other smells, and Samuel winced, remembering the smoke rising from his own smoldering skin. He rubbed his arm where the lumpy scar marked his servitude to the master at his dig. He hated taking advantage of someone else's misery, but as long as the master was busy with the new arrivals, his chances of escaping were better. He bolted down a passageway, his feet splattering mud.

He ran until he reached the edge of camp, then slammed into a stone-and-iron barricade. To his surprise, it rattled loosely. He brushed his hands over the surface, and instead of metal and rock, he touched rickety, splintered wood. Excitement rushed through him. It was just as

Macduff had explained: the anesthetizing hana berry juice created a false reality.

If he had only known how easy it was to escape, he could have returned home long before. Without another thought, he punched his fist through the slats. The wood shattered as pain shot up his arm.

He peered through the hole, sucking the blood on his knuckles. He saw the rocky hill a short distance away, exactly as Macduff had described it.

His father had warned him that he was too fearless and needed to temper his bravery with caution, but tonight he hoped his boldness would serve him well. He pushed through the opening. The boards cracked and split apart. Long splinters dug into skin and broke off, leaving quills in his back. He ran across the bare ground, his feet slapping the hard-packed dirt. He reached the hill and waited, breathless, to see if he had been followed.

When nothing happened, he began climbing the sharp incline and thought about the dangers he would face at home. When he'd left his family's homestead, the Shawnee, Mingo, and Miami had been at war with the pioneers, who had been breaking the treaties and invading the western valleys. He hoped that once he escaped he would emerge in the hills near his parents' cabin. He knew how to survive in that wilderness. He could walk without leaving a track and blend into the forest without being seen. But he feared that instead he might find himself in unfamiliar territory, stranded in the dead of winter.

Samuel reached the crest and stood at the edge of a forest, breathing the fresh pine scent. Nefandus had an artificial sky that hid the moon because the residents despised the lunar glow and hated the feel of its luminescence on their skin. Instead, lurid red stars lit the moonless sky, and their scarlet light cast a crimson blush over the shadows lurking in front of him.

Macduff had told him to continue to the ocean, so he pressed through the spreading branches and followed a trail marked with stacked stones and tridents cut into tree bark. Dry cones and pine needles crackled beneath his footsteps. He had gone only a short distance when he was overcome by a feeling that something was following him. But when he looked back, he saw nothing except forest, frosted with an eerie red radiance.

At last he found himself at the edge of a sea cliff. Wind rushed through his hair, and the ocean brine mixed with the dank smells from the woods behind him.

He braced himself against a rock and glanced down. Surf crashed over the craggy shore, churning the brooding sea into white foam. Macduff had told him to dive off the precipice, but now he wasn't sure he had that kind of courage. Maybe his father had been wrong about him after all, or perhaps living as a slave in Nefandus had dampened his brave pioneer spirit.

He untied a pocket watch knotted in the rags draped around his waist. The gold case glittered in the starlight. Macduff had given it to him the night he had left. Now Samuel opened it, amazed again by what he saw. Instead of keeping time, the face showed earth's sky.

He turned the dial. Sun, moon, planets, and stars moved beneath the crystal. He stopped on a familiar grouping of stars. The gate between Nefandus and earth opened only when the eye of Medusa within the constellation of Perseus blinked. The star's brightness had already dimmed. It was time to jump.

But he didn't see anything below him that appeared to be an opening between two dimensions, only jagged rocks. He had expected to see a shimmer or a freakish arc of light.

He hesitated. Like most *servi*, he couldn't die. The master had given him immortality not as a gift but because slaves were more valuable if they lived forever, frozen in youth. Yet looking down at the sharp outcroppings, he knew there were fates worse than death. If the stories Macduff had told about the gateway weren't true, then Samuel would hit the hard shore and live for an eternity as a pool of blood and shattered bone. He thought about turning to shadow and floating down, but Macduff's instructions had been clear; he had to go through the portal in solid form.

Samuel clasped the watch and spread his arms, determined. But as he eased onto his toes to push off, it occurred to him that he didn't know where Macduff had gotten his information. What if his knowledge were no more than rumor, spread by *servi* to give each other hope?

Again he paused. He desperately wanted to see his family again. How long had it been? He wasn't sure. His recent past was a blur. The hana berry juice had made his mind foggy. Now Samuel was clearheaded, and, with that clarity of perception, he knew only a fool would try to escape by plunging off this cliff. He opened the watch again and stared at the constellation. He had waited too long; the gate between the two realms, if it really did exist, was closing; the star was regaining its brilliance.

A pinecone snapped behind him and his breath caught. Something rustled through the dry grass. He looked over his shoulder. A shadow threaded sinuously around the tree trunks. Then a mountain lion came into view, slinking stealthily forward, its belly low to the ground.

"Lord of the forest," Samuel whispered reverentially, using the name his great-grandfather had given the beast. It had been the elderly man's power animal, and now Samuel stood transfixed, overcome by its majesty and terrible beauty. This one was unlike any he had seen before; its silver eyes seemed sentient and filled with wisdom.

The giant cat crouched, hind muscles taut, ready to spring. Usually silent, it twisted its head and uttered a shrill, piercing whistle, a sound it made only when cornered. But what alarmed it now?

Without warning, it lunged, claws spread. The powerful paws hit Samuel's chest and pushed him off the cliff. He plummeted down, the wind shrieking around him, louder than his screams. He ignored Macduff's warning and tried to turn to shadow and stop his fall, but adrenaline surged through his muscles and made him too nervous to transform. The other *servi* were right. Escape was impossible. He was going to hit the jagged rocks and live, a bloody mess of flesh and broken bones.

CHAPTER TWO

SUDDENLY THE seacoast blurred, sound stopped, and the ocean spray stood still, a white lace against the black sky. A sticky web enveloped Samuel and held him suspended above the rocky shore. He gasped and the gluey film spread into his mouth, coating his tongue and gagging him. Before he could cough it out, his body went numb. Macduff hadn't warned him about this. Maybe he had fallen into a trap used to catch escaping *servi*.

He feared he would remain in this tomblike stillness for eternity, but just as panic set in, a sharp chill cut through him and, without warning, he was released from the web. He braced himself, preparing to slam onto the spiky rocks below, but instead he hit soft, cold sand. He lay there, breathing fast and deeply, staring at the long line of flat beach. Had he passed through after all?

The soothing rhythm of the surf filled the cool night. A foamy wave rushed onto shore, and its icy water caressed his ankles, then drifted back. He lifted his head. A full moon graced the heavens, huge and opalescent. Happiness raced through him. He must be home. The ocean was far from his family's cabin, but he could find his way back to the frontier easily enough.

Disoriented and giddy, he stood and stumbled into the breakers. His clumsiness made him laugh. Already his mind was gathering stories to tell his younger brothers and sisters. But how much time had passed? A year, maybe two? It could easily have been five. They might be married already, with children. He tried to fix his mind on the joy of being an uncle, but another thought pushed through and saddened him. If he married, his wife and offspring would age but he'd remain forever fifteen.

He shook the worry away. Macduff would have the answers. Right now he needed to celebrate. He whooped and charged into the phosphorescent waves. He licked the salty spray from his lips, relishing the briny taste. He started to dive under a swell and then stopped, overcome by what he saw in the sky. Four stars skimmed across the horizon in descending formation, blinking red and white. He'd seen shooting stars before, but never any that moved so slowly.

Before he could consider that mystery, something much more menacing caught his eye. Three black shadows sped over the incoming surf. The sleek silhouettes had to be Regulators: powerful ones sent from Nefandus to bring back Renegades. Fear seized him, and his stomach muscles tightened.

He sprinted across the wet shoreline, leaping over glistening piles of kelp, and headed away from the breakwater to the pale, dry sand. He willed his body to fade. Macduff had told him his ability to transform would work here, but when nothing happened, he assumed

Macduff had been wrong, and he quickened his pace.

A shadow swooped in front of him. The inky cloud formed into a human shape and a guy his age dropped down. His long blond hair billowed in the breeze, his baggy clothes flapping about his body.

"We've come to help you." He offered his hand, his skin so pale it glowed in the moonlight. "I'm Omer. They call me Obie. I'm a Renegade like you, a Son of the Dark."

Samuel didn't trust him; Regulators disguised themselves when they visited earth. He turned and ran, but a black smudge streamed alongside him. It molded into a tall figure with short, spiked hair. The guy leaped forward and caught him, but then let go, his nose wrinkling as if he had smelled something foul.

"Get him, Kyle," Obie ordered, frustration rising in his voice. "We need him."

"He stinks." Kyle shook his head. "And where's he going to go?"

"Damn it." Obie started chasing after him again.

Samuel nervously scanned the beach, not sure which way to go. He twisted about and bumped into a third guy, who had materialized behind him. They had him penned now.

"Man, you are seriously going to end up on *Style Court* looking like that," the last one said.

"Berto, we don't have time for jokes," Obie said.

Berto folded his arms over his chest in annoyance. His black hair blew into his eyes. "Would you ease up? We got him now. Everything's going to be okay."

Samuel studied the three. He didn't think they were Regulators, even though he could sense Berto's evil percolating close to the surface. They smelled too clean, of soap and spice, and the air didn't hum with that terrible vibration.

"Are you sure he's the right one?" Kyle asked. "The autumnal equinox is still a couple of weeks away."

"The runes said tonight," Obie explained, stepping closer.

"Maybe someone else is coming through."

Kyle stared at Samuel as if he were a cockroach.

But Samuel sensed they were as nervous as he was, and he wondered why. Surely they weren't afraid of him.

Berto pointed to the sky. "Mars is aligned with the full moon. Tezcatlipoca said the fourth one would come through then—"

"Great." Kyle ran his hands over his head. "We're relying on a bag of stones and an ancient god with a smoking mirror to decide our future. Does that seem smart, considering what we're up against?"

Samuel looked them over and imagined he could break free. He was sure he could outrun them and get to the bluffs before they even had time to change to shadow. He only needed one small distraction. He eased back.

"The mirror sees the future," Berto argued. "When I looked at it, I was given clairvoyance." He pointed at Samuel. "I saw him on this beach."

Kyle looked doubtful. "This guy? With all the dirt on his face how can you tell he's the right one? You said yourself the mirror's surface was like smoke—"

"I said the mirror was made from obsidian—black volcanic glass—and it reflects darkly and sometimes with distortions, but I know what I saw," Berto said. "He's the fourth."

"What do you mean, 'the fourth'?" Samuel pretended to take part in the conversation, while he focused on getting away.

Kyle ignored his question. "At best he's a misfit, or a Regulator disguising as a runaway."

"He escaped the digs," Berto answered. "You weren't in Nefandus long enough to know what life could be like there."

"Ignore Kyle," Obie said and touched Samuel's shoulder.

Samuel jerked back, and threw a punch at Obie's mouth. His knuckles scraped against teeth, cutting his own skin. Obie stumbled, surprised, then steadied himself, but before he could swing, Samuel spun around and raced away.

Their footsteps pounded after him.

"Wait!" Obie yelled. "You can't survive without us."

A thunderclap shattered the night, the sound reverberating down the shore.

"Regulators broke through!" Berto yelled in warning. "You need to come with us, Samuel."

Samuel. How did Berto know his name? Had his god Tezcatlipoca told him that as well? Samuel glanced back but didn't slow his pace.

A sudden gust blasted around him, stirring the sand into a funnel. Monstrous figures dropped from the churning air and hit the beach with a solid thump, forming a barricade in front of Samuel. Two creatures formed, looking roughly human, their features hard and exaggerated; the energy buzzing around them, was unmistakable. They were Regulators. They continued to solidify, becoming handsome imitations of mortals. Their eyes locked onto his.

Samuel froze. He couldn't trust the Regulators tromping toward him, but he didn't trust the three who called themselves Sons of the Dark, either.

"Run!" Kyle was already transparent, his ghostly shape undulating in the ocean breeze.

"Follow us and you'll be safe!" Obie shouted. His body evaporated into a murky phantom and whipped away.

"What are you waiting for? Turn to shadow. Your powers work here," Berto said, lingering longer than the other two before he turned into a blurry outline of himself and disappeared in a plume of smoke.

Samuel faded, but instead of following the others, he flew in the opposite direction. As a shadow his vision was panoramic and now he had an unbroken view of the entire shore. A fast-moving fog streaked after him, Regulators hidden within its mists.

Ahead light blazed on the horizon. He hoped it was a settlement. He had heard that the eastern states had large cities, but as he glided up the embankment, the night exploded with deafening gunfire, whoops, cries, and screams, reminding him of the first moments of battle. The light must have been coming from a fort under siege.

He soared over a block wall, expecting to see a fierce fight below. Instead, shock made him materialize. He plummeted to the ground and landed in a crouch, not understanding the spectacle in front of him. Where was he?

CHAPTER THREE

SAMUEL STOOD dumbfounded, a heavy drumbeat pulsing through him. Kids his age faced an empty stage, screaming, their hands high above their heads, pounding the air in cadence with the driving rhythm.

Three guys ran onstage and began playing instruments that resembled guitars, only these were triangular and painted brash colors. A girl with pink hair joined them and sang, her voice more snarl than melody.

Then he sensed a disturbance, one more deadly than the barrage of noise. Thin black threads spread sinuously over the audience, winding down and searching. Regulators had found him.

Samuel ran through the narrow space between two buildings. He twisted, wiggled, and struggled to the other side, then hurried to the embankment and skidded down the slope. He sprinted back to the beach where he'd fallen through the portal, hoping to find a clue to guide him.

He stood in the moonlight and slowly turned. He had followed Macduff's instructions, or at least he'd thought he had, but something had gone wrong. Maybe he had never left Nefandus after all.

In the distance, a wooden staircase led up from the beach. He hurried to it, then paused, breathless. Someone had scratched a trident into one of the balustrades. Was this the path he should have followed?

Cautiously, he climbed the creaking steps, fearful the noise would bring the Regulators back. At the top he followed a walkway to a hard flat surface in front of a low-lying building with a door large enough for a barn.

Exhausted, he surrendered, and lay down on the slab. How was he ever going to get home to his family now?

A deep rumbling made him sit up. Two columns of light bore down on him. He squinted against the glare. A sudden raucous noise like the squawk from a wild goose made him jump up.

"What the—"

The twin beams crept forward, emanating from two circles attached to a smooth gleaming surface. He tentatively pressed his hands over the warm glossy shell. What was this thing? Then through the brightness he saw a girl looking at him. Immediately, a door opened in the side of the machine and she stepped out, her long blond hair curling over her shoulders.

She strolled toward him, unafraid, her eyes daring him to touch her. "You stupid nitwit, don't you know to get out of the way of a car?"

"That's what you call this contraption?" he asked, studying her.

Her boots had heels at least three inches high. How practical was that? Samuel's eyes traveled up her bare knees, over her thighs. She must have forgotten to put on her skirt. That was just fine with him. Not everything was bad about this place. He smiled foolishly.

"You're in my way," she said impatiently. "Can you move? I need to get into my garage."

Her tone implied that he was a dunce, but her lips puckered in a saucy way that made him want to bend down and kiss her. He wished he were wearing his best buckskins and not the loincloth all *servi* wore.

"I'm so sick of homeless people thinking they can camp out in my driveway. So, what do you want? Twenty dollars to leave and never come back?" She scowled, and then something caught her eye. She grabbed his arm and studied his branding scar. Her long, red-painted fingernails traced over it. She looked up at him, puzzled.

A spark crackled over her hair, and then in the shadows behind her a darkness grew, like vents of steam, intertwining and binding. She didn't seem aware of the hulking shapes.

"What is it?" she asked nervously, as if she had read the fear on his face.

Macduff had warned him not to let anyone see him use his powers, but he couldn't desert the girl and allow the Regulators to take her back to Nefandus as a slave.

He dove at her. Her eyes widened and her mouth opened in a scream, but he had already wrapped his arms around her. Her body shriveled into vapor, her skin and bones transformed by his power. He coiled around her and soared, carrying her with him.

The Regulators drew together into a sinister, pitch-black mass and shot after them. Samuel zigzagged around buildings and trees, then down into foul-smelling, dank places beneath the street, and finally up through a grid, soaring high again over the ocean.

The girl groaned, restless, and tried to wrench free.

"It's all right," he whispered.

But that didn't stop her squirming.

"If you try to break away from me now, you'll fall." He struggled to hold her, but if he didn't land quickly she was going to slip through his grasp, materialize, and plunge into the water.

He wasn't sure if he had outdistanced the Regulators yet, but he couldn't risk hurting her. He floated into a rising fog bank, then settled on a pier near a small bait-and-tackle shop. Their bodies remolded under a circle of tawny light.

"Sorry," he said and relaxed. "I hope I didn't scare you, but I had to protect—"

"My boots!" She shoved him hard and jumped back, stomping. "You set me in a puddle of fish guts. These are Prada! Do you know how much I paid for them?"

"You're worried about your boots?" He stared at her, baffled. "Don't you understand what just happened to you?"

"Ruined," she mumbled. "And look what you've done to my outfit."

She started walking away, her steps pounding hollowly on the tarred boards, and Samuel followed close behind. "This dress was an original, and now it smells like I slept with a skunk. I don't even have my perfume with me. It's in my purse, in my car, and both are probably stolen by now." She spun around and tried to punch him, but he dodged the blow.

"Where I come from we thank a man for saving our life," he said indignantly.

"You're just a *servus* from the digs," she said, stomping down the pier. "This is going to be harder than I thought. I'll have to educate you."

"How do you know what I am?" He grabbed her hand, and she flinched.

"The brand on your arm," she said, trying to pull away. "You're not what I expected to see come through tonight."

"How did so many people know I was coming through when I didn't even know myself?" he asked anxiously.

"You've met others?" Now he had her full attention. The apprehension on her face matched what he was feeling.

"You answer my question first," he said and dropped his hold. "How'd you know I was escaping tonight?"

"Astronomy," she whispered reverentially, and gazed at the fog-clotted sky. "The stars said the fourth one would come through tonight."

"Fourth one?" he asked, perturbed.

Her mood softened. "You don't know, do you?"

"It doesn't matter much what I know," he said, infuriated by the pity in her eyes. "Just point me toward the frontier on the Ohio River. I need to get home."

"I'll take you," she said and held out her hand.

Could he trust her? He hesitated and then reached for her. But as he did, Berto appeared, materializing so rapidly he created a breeze. "Don't touch her, Samuel."

"I already have," Samuel answered.

"Ashley's dangerous." Berto stood between them. "This is what we were trying to warn you about." He spoke to Samuel but his gaze kept returning to Ashley. "You can't trust all the people on this side."

"If there's anyone you can't trust, it's Berto," Ashley countered angrily. "He's not what he seems. Does he look like a *servus*?"

Samuel agreed with her observation. "But you don't either," he said honestly.

Ashley pulled her top off her shoulder, revealing beautiful, tanned skin marked with the ugly brand of the trident. Then Samuel noticed thin white scars on her knuckles. The little finger on her left hand looked as if it had been broken and had healed badly.

"You're one?" he asked, not expecting an answer. No wonder she hadn't been startled when he'd turned her to shadow.

She held out her hand again, daring Berto to stop her. "Come with me, Samuel. I'm the only one who can take you home."

"I don't trust either one of you." Samuel fell back and vanished into the fog. He slipped beneath the pier, and wrapped around a barnacle-encrusted piling, listening to their voices above him.

"See what you've done now," Ashley said harshly. "I hate you, Berto. Why can't you leave me alone?"

"Don't try to take him from us," Berto threatened.

CHAPTER FOUR

SAMUEL DRIFTED WITH the fog. The roiling mists chilled him and the tranquil slowness soothed him. Macduff had warned him not to trust anyone, and already he had almost gone with Ashley. He wasn't sure if that would have been a mistake or not, but he had to be more careful. Right now he needed to find shelter before the Regulators caught up to him again. Macduff had said to hide in hallowed ground—any holy place where the Good in the universe was worshipped. He'd be safe from Regulators there.

In the distance a steeple poked through the churning vapors. He sailed down and slipped between broken panes in a stained-glass window. Weary and shivering, his body gathered together. The church was abandoned and smelled of mouse droppings and mold.

The charred remains of a campfire blackened the bare floor. Someone had used the church for refuge before him. Maybe Macduff had sat here, or perhaps other *servi* had found shelter within these walls.

He flopped down on a pew and rested his feet on a pile of yellowed newspapers. A heading caught his eye. He leaned forward. His back stiffened and then collapsed, his lungs releasing a slow, wretched moan.

Los Angeles Times was inscribed on the top border, but it was the date below the heading that made his heart jump. He clutched the brittle paper and held it up to better light.

The hana berry juice had made his mind groggy, but could he have been in such a stupor that he hadn't noticed decades rushing by? If this date was correct, then two hundred years had passed since he'd been kidnapped and taken to Nefandus. Was he standing now in the twenty-first century?

CHAPTER FIVE

SAMUEL AWAKENED repeatedly during the night, each time praying he had somehow been catapulted back to the frontier, but when he stepped to the window in the choir loft, he stared out at the same three lights changing from red to green to yellow and back to red. This time, he surrendered to his insomnia and read the newspapers. By the time the sparrows had begun chattering with the dawn, he had made a decision.

He had survived in Nefandus with the hope of being reunited with his family, and he wasn't going to abandon that goal now. Obie, Kyle, and Berto had promised to protect him, but

Ashley had offered to take him back to his home. Macduff's warning came back to him, and he brushed it away. Ashley was his only chance; he didn't care what price he had to pay.

He needed to find her, but first he had to get something to wear. He tromped over scattered hymnals to a door behind the altar and opened it. Across the back lot, clothes flapped lazily on a rope drawn from a boxy blue house to the skeletal branches of a dead tree.

Silently, he crept across the parched grass and stole a pair of pink slacks and a white shirt. He dashed back, making a mental promise to pay the person for what he had taken as soon as he could.

Inside the church he stripped off his loincloth and pulled on the baggy slacks, cinching the drawstring around his hips. He stuffed Macduff's watch into a pocket, slipped into the shirt, then ventured outside and strode barefoot down the sidewalk.

Cars rumbled past, speeding in both directions, one crowded next to the other, chuffing and churning smoke. Horns blared.

People seemed to be in foul, frowning moods, their eyes hidden behind thick black lenses. Overhead wires bridged the sidewalk, hanging from poles.

"This is one sorry world," he said, wondering what had happened to the forests.

Immediately, his neck and spine tickling, as if someone were watching him. He turned and saw a raven sweep down, cawing loudly. Its sleek black wings shimmered in the sunlight. His great-grandpa Elijah had called the bird good luck, a sign of protection, but Macduff had feared the raven, telling Samuel it was a messenger from the dark side.

Samuel wasn't superstitious. He grinned and recited the incantation Elijah had taught him. "I willingly pass through the doorway into the dark realm of the raven."

Abruptly pain raced through his arms, and his elbows shot up as if forming wings. His skin prickled with spiny bumps.

"I take it back!" he shouted and nervously forced his hands to his sides. Elijah had warned him not to say the words until he understood their power. He glanced up and started to laugh. Hunger and lack of sleep had caused the strange sensation, not magic, but then he remembered that a churchwoman had once accused Elijah of changing into a bird. Was that possible?

The raven cackled impatiently, then flapped its wings and took to the sky again.

Samuel sprinted after it.

Two blocks later the bird rounded a corner and perched on a wire. Samuel caught up to it and found himself in a crowd of young people. *Turney High School* was painted on the side of a beige building.

"I've been looking for you," a voice called.

Samuel turned and the bird flew away, a swirling silver radiance trailing after it

Ashley walked toward him, slow and easy. She wore a glittering white jewel in her belly button and black leggings.

"I followed you over here last night," she said. "But then I lost you. Usually guys hang around waiting for me. I was hoping you would." She started to touch him and drew back. "Even more I was hoping you would have bathed by now."

"I would have if I could have found a lake or stream." He couldn't take his eyes off her.

"You can shower in the locker room. Follow me." Ashley shoved through the groups of loitering students, and led him to a large building.

He followed her inside. Voices echoed around him as if he were in a cavern, and the moist air smelled of sweat and soap.

"This is the football team," Ashley explained. "They start working out at four in the morning and continue through first period."

"Dang, Ashley, what are you doing?" A muscular guy grabbed a bright orange shirt with a large black *31* written across the front and wrapped it around his waist.

"Please, Sledge," Ashley fired back. "If I had wanted to see you naked, I could have thought of a better way to do it."

The two guys standing near Sledge burst into laughter.

"Shut up, Barry," Sledge said, his green eyes narrowing. Spiky tattoos circled his biceps.

"I wasn't laughing." Barry stood bare-chested, his neck as thick as a bull's.

Sledge turned his irritation back to Ashley. "You can't bring a homeless guy into the locker room. He's probably got fleas."

Ashley ignored Sledge and kept walking. "Don't worry about Sledge," she said over her shoulder to Samuel. "He won't do anything. He's totally crushing on me even though he's dating Allison."

Ashley stepped aside and Samuel caught his reflection in a mirror. He moved closer, stunned, not believing the image was his own, yet knowing it had to be. Dirt matted his hair and caked his face. He had been handsome once. Girls had giggled behind their hands when he was around. Bolder ones had even asked him to dance at the church socials.

"You are definitely going to be a challenge." Ashley opened the door to a small cubical. "But I work miracles."

He stepped into the stall, turned and stared at her. "What now?"

"Don't you know anything? They do have showers in Nefandus after all." She grabbed a round silver knob. "This is a spigot. Turn it, and *voilà*."

Hot water splashed over him. He flinched, startled at first, then appreciatively held his face up to the spray.

Ashley handed him a white bar. "Soap," she explained. "And by the way, you're wearing girls' pajama bottoms. I'll see if I can find something for you to put on." She closed the door.

He carefully put the pocket watch on a shelf, then stripped from his clothes, and began washing.

Before too long a piercing voice made him turn off the water. Ashley poked her head into the steam and gave him a withering look. "You've been in there twenty minutes, okay?" She handed him a towel and closed the door.

He draped it around his hips and stepped out, taking the watch with him.

Ashley looked at him differently now. She stepped closer and stared up at him, letting the water from his hair, chin, and nose drip onto her blouse.

"Aren't you worried about your fancy clothes getting wet?" he teased.

"I'll buy more." She picked up a pair of faded jeans and a blue shirt from the bench. "Try these. I snatched them from Lost and Found."

He set the watch down, waited for her to turn around, grabbed the jeans and pulled them on.

"I'll tell you everything you need to know," she promised. "I help Followers and *servi* who want to escape. I show them how to adjust to life here. It's not easy."

"I don't need to learn," he said bluntly. "I'm going back to the frontier where I belong." He stared down at the fly, searching for the buttons. Metal teeth lined either side of the opening. He glanced up.

Ashley was watching him. Had she been the whole time?

"It's called a zipper," she explained, and boldly grabbed the metal tab. She pulled it up. "See? You do need me. You only have two choices for now. You can go back to Nefandus, or you can adjust to living in Los Angeles."

"Last night you gave me a third choice," he challenged. "You said you'd take me home."

She shrugged. "Maybe you'll get used to this new world and like it better."

"From what I've seen, I don't think so," he said, but her sly look told him she was used to getting her way.

"Come on." She eased her hands around the crook of his arm and led him outside.

The morning sun beat hot on his face. His toes clenched the dew-wet grass. A raven circled over head, cawing. He wondered if it were the same one.

Ashley caught him watching the bird. "You really don't have a clue, do you?" she asked and stopped in front of a silver car.

Samuel forgot the bird and ran his hand over the smooth metal.

"It's a Corvette," she said proudly, as if

that should mean something to him. She jingled her keys, then pressed one. A small beep followed. "Get in."

Ashley opened his door and the bird's shadow swept over them.

Just as quickly a rugged, tanned hand reached past her and closed the door.

Samuel whipped around, alarmed.

Obie, Berto, and Kyle stood behind him, looking grim.

"We've all fallen for Ashley," Berto said, giving the impression he hadn't gotten over his fall yet. "It's hard not to, but you'll regret it if you go with her."

Ashley smiled, seeming to derive pleasure from Berto's pained expression.

"Haven't you figured out what she is yet?" Obie asked. "She's a *venatrix*."

Samuel's stomach churned. He'd heard stories about the *venatores*—bounty hunters, *servi* who had escaped but now worked with Regulators, hunting down Renegades and taking them back to Nefandus for a reward. He glanced at Ashley.

She didn't deny the accusation.

"She's been waiting for you," Kyle added and glared at her. "She thinks you're the fourth, and she hopes if she can take you back to Nefandus she'll be given enough power to return to her own time."

"What's this 'fourth' you keep talking about?" Samuel asked. He tried to sound calm, but his heart was racing. Was traveling back in time possible? If Ashley didn't have the power yet, then perhaps these three did. Maybe they really were Sons of the Dark. If so, could they help him return home?

"We'll explain everything to you," Obie said and offered his hand. "Come with us."

Samuel hesitated, not sure he could trust anyone.

"Do any of you know a *servus* named Macduff?" Ashley asked casually.

"What about Macduff?" Samuel's heart felt as if it would explode.

Ashley didn't look up. She leaned seductively against her car, staring into a small mirror cupped in her palm. She rubbed glossy red color on her lips and let him wait for her answer.

"He's staying with me," she said finally and snapped the mirror closed. She tossed her hair. "I thought you might like to see him." She grinned, knowing she had won.

CHAPTER SIX

ON THE FRONTIER Samuel had had to rely on his instincts to survive, and right now every part of his being was thrumming, warning him not to trust Ashley. He climbed into her car anyway.

Berto smacked the roof of the car with his hand, his defeat unbearable. "We might not be able to rescue you," he warned. "You don't know what she can do to you," he said regretfully. Then he caught Ashley watching him and stepped back.

"You're the fourth," Obie continued. "It's not just about you. Others. . . ."

Kyle pulled on his arm. "Don't explain that here." He looked around, worried someone might be listening.

"It's not that I want to go with her," Samuel said, his own sense of foreboding growing. "But I don't have a choice." He looked at Berto with an apologetic expression. "Macduff is my friend."

"Whatever, man," Berto said, and then he kicked the door closed.

"I'll come back with him," Samuel muttered, trying to make peace. "And then we'll talk."

"Ignore them." Ashley slid into the car seat beside Samuel. "They're jealous, you know, of you and me. I guess you can tell that Berto and I were once involved."

"Involved in what?" he asked, anxious to see Macduff.

"In each other," she answered, as if sharing that secret would impress him. "You know?"

He felt certain he did know, and her confession made a blush rise to his cheeks, even though she didn't seem embarrassed.

"It's over," she said sweetly, her eyes intense and inviting.

"Are you telling me this for a reason?" he asked.

"The way you looked at me," she said, and let her hand slide over his knee. "I thought you'd want to know."

"No," he answered honestly. "What you do is your own business, and I'd appreciate it if you'd keep it to yourself."

Her confident expression vanished, replaced with the perplexed look of a predator who'd been outsmarted by its prey. Then a devious grin crossed her lips. "Really?" She slipped a pair of black-lens glasses over her eyes. "I don't believe you."

She slammed her foot on the pedal and the car roared forward.

He felt her watching him. He suspected she was hoping to unnerve him, but his attention was focused on a more pressing problem. Even if he did bring Macduff back to this part of town, how was he going to find Berto, Obie, and Kyle again? They hadn't told him where they lived.

What made him think he could trust them any more than he could trust Ashley? He had to go it alone. That was the only way for now.

The car stopped suddenly with a loud squeal and he fell forward, almost hitting his head on the windshield. People crossed the street in front of them.

"We have got to get you some sunglasses." Ashley opened a compartment above his knees and grabbed a pair. "These looked totally cool on the last guy I dated." She sat up and adjusted them on the bridge of his nose, letting her fingers wander into his hair.

A car honked behind them. She fell back in her seat, and the car rammed forward.

"Do you think you can trust Berto?" she asked finally, breaking her silence. She steered into the drive where Samuel had met her the night before.

"Maybe," he answered.

The car stopped and she lifted her glasses. "At least I admit I'm a bounty hunter." She paused. "That's something to consider when you're deciding who to trust."

"Are you telling me they're bounty hunters, too?" He climbed from the car.

"Come on." She got out, ran ahead of him, and ignoring his question, unlocked the pale blue door to a house.

He followed her inside. The view of the ocean from the windows made him take off his glasses for a better look. "It's beautiful," he said, watching the seagulls and the waves.

"You could have a place like this on the beach," she said slyly.

"Yeah," he agreed glumly. "I suppose if it were something I wanted."

She disappeared down a short hallway, closed a door and came back, then kicked off her shoes and strode barefoot behind a tiled counter near a table cluttered with books.

"I bet you're starved," she said. "I am."

"You're studying up on the frontier?" He lifted a book and eagerly thumbed through the pages, then opened a second one on astrology. Someone had carefully marked a chapter on the autumnal equinox with a red ribbon.

"The autumnal equinox?" he asked,

thinking back to the night before. Kyle had also mentioned it. "What's so important about that day?"

She took his hand, clearly trying to distract him, and pulled him behind the counter with her. "I told you. I study the stars to see the future." She opened the door to a large rectangular box in the corner. "Let's eat something."

Cool air struck him and he looked at her, surprised.

"It's a refrigerator," she said. "In Nefandus we used magic to do everything. Here, we use electricity."

He gazed hungrily at the apples and potatoes on the shelves. She pulled out a pack of smooth reddish tubes.

"You'll love these." She pushed around him and opened another white cubicle. This one was smaller and sat on the counter. She set two tubes inside on a glass plate.

"It's a microwave." She closed the door and pressed several buttons.

Humming followed, and a delicious, spicy smell made his stomach grumble.

The box beeped and she pulled out the food, steaming now with juice bubbling over the skin.

"What kind of sausages are those?" he asked, his mouth watering.

"Just wait." She curled bread around one, and handed it to him. "Enjoy your hot dog."

He dropped it. "I'll starve before I eat a dog."

She laughed. "First, you have to learn not to take everything you hear literally. Hot dogs are the best food ever invented, and no dog was ever killed to make one." She took a bite of hers, then offered it to him.

He put half of it into his mouth and savored the salty taste. She stayed close, watching him eat, her breath soft and warm. He swallowed and looked at her, his body telling him one thing, his mind another.

"Where's Macduff?" he whispered, trying to break the spell she had cast over him.

"He'll be here soon enough." She pulled out a chair and motioned for Samuel to sit at the table next to her. "Right now we have to

go over a few basics, so you'll know how to survive here. First I need to show you how to
shave."

By the time she had finished, three empty
cartons of ice cream lined the counter. She had
taken him into the bathroom and taught him
how to use the modern conveniences, and in the
kitchen she had instructed him on working
the appliances. But best of all, he had liked her
plasma TV. He was still rummaging through
her refrigerator when she came over and
caressed his arm.

"We've finished for today." Ashley took his
hand and pulled him onto the balcony. Rain
pelted the roof and the sand. The downpour
had started sometime during the afternoon.

Falling stars blinked, descending below the
clouds, but now he knew the lights came from
airplanes landing at Los Angeles International
Airport.

Ashley faced him and put her hands on his
chest. "You'll get used to this world," she whispered.

"Maybe I don't want to," he answered.

Sudden homesickness made a lump in his throat.

"Do you really want to leave a place with so much to offer?" She held her face up to his, as if waiting for a kiss.

"It's time we found Macduff," he said and eased back.

"Aren't you having a good time with me?" She guided his hands around her waist.

"I came here because you said Macduff was staying with you." He took his hands back and folded his arms over his chest.

"He's in the bedroom," she said peevishly and stomped inside. She plopped down into a large chair, picked up the remote, and started surfing through the TV channels.

Samuel ignored her bad mood. His anger was building, too. "You should have told me he was here."

She shrugged.

He walked down the short hallway to the door. He didn't think but just pushed his way inside. A sour smell enveloped him. He swallowed hard to keep the food in his stomach.

"Macduff?" He hurried across the thick carpeting to the tangle of blankets on the bed. "Hey, are you in there?" he asked. "It's me. Samuel."

When Macduff didn't answer he tentatively pulled back the covers. Macduff lay curled in a ball.

"I'm sorry you followed me out," Macduff whispered without looking up. His lips were dry and parched.

"Those weren't exactly the words I had expected to hear from you," Samuel said and sat on the edge of the bed. He could feel the warmth radiating from Macduff's body and wondered if he had a fever. "Have you been sick?"

Macduff uncurled and rolled away from him.

"Things will get better now." Samuel clasped his friend's shoulder. "We've got each other, so it won't be so lonely."

"You're a fool if you think that's going to be enough to make things right here," Macduff said angrily. "Don't you know yet?"

"Sure I do," Samuel answered, trying to think of a way to bolster Macduff's spirits.

"Time went by while we were in Nefandus."

"We don't fit in this world anymore," Macduff said. "We never will again."

"We continue to be fifteen forever," Samuel said, as if it weren't a problem. "We can handle that. When all our friends start to age, we'll just move on, so people won't start wondering about us. And even if they do figure it out, this world is crazy. I bet they won't even do anything about it. They'll probably help us sell our blood to rich old ladies who want to use it for a wrinkle cream. We'll be . . . *stars*." Samuel used the new term uneasily. "That's what Ashley said anyway."

Macduff didn't laugh at his attempt at humor. Instead he frowned. "You don't even know what I'm talking about."

"We discussed it before you escaped," Samuel continued, feeling despair gather in his chest. "If you live forever it means you eventually have to bury your own kids. But I've been thinking hard on that one. If the master made us immortal, then someone in Nefandus has got to know how to make us mortal again."

Macduff snorted dismissively. "We've already lived two hundred years," he argued. "If they change us back now we'll be nothing but dust and bones."

Samuel never thought things through the way Macduff did. He always acted and paid the price for his recklessness, and right now he wanted to take Macduff and get away. He didn't like being so close to the portal or to a *venatrix*. He also had a growing fear that Berto, Obie, and Kyle might return, and he didn't know if he could trust them.

"I know it's bad. But we can adjust," Samuel said at last, wishing his voice sounded more optimistic.

"I told you," Macduff said bitterly. "We can't live in this world. Do you know what happens if you try to kiss someone here who isn't one of us?"

"Kiss someone?" Samuel felt confused. He wasn't sure if Macduff was trying to make a joke or not, but he fell easily into their old, teasing relationship. "I only arrived last night. Are you telling me you got a girl already?"

"I killed her," Macduff whispered, his lips trembling with the confession.

"What?" Samuel leaned closer, certain he had misunderstood.

"I didn't mean to," Macduff went on. "I liked her, loved her maybe. She made me feel like I had a chance at a new life. A couple of times, I had to make some lame excuse so we could escape the Regulators, but I could even feel their interest in me fading. It's not like I was anyone important."

"What do you mean, you killed her?" Samuel asked anxiously.

"I kissed her," Macduff mumbled into the pillow. "She collapsed in my arms."

"I bet she just fainted. You probably squeezed her too hard," Samuel said.

"No. Something happened inside me, like I was . . ." Macduff stopped and started again. "You remember how they looked *after*, when the master took us hunting?

"Have you seen her since you kissed her?" Samuel asked, not wanting to believe. "Maybe we should go see her."

"I don't have the courage," Macduff said. "I heard from friends that she was ill and the doctors didn't know what was wrong with her. I drew her life away just like we did when the master made us—" He couldn't bring himself to say the contemptible thing they had been forced to do. The master had called it "hunting."

"Just like a vampire," Macduff went on, his voice barely audible. "Only I didn't take any blood, just"—he shuddered—"her soul. Is that what we were doing all those times the master took us hunting? Stealing souls?"

"Maybe that's how the master kept us immortal," Samuel said and his shoulders slumped. "Or at least strong enough to work in the digs."

"By making us feed on others?" Macduff asked.

Samuel didn't answer. What they had done had terrified him, but he had also derived intense pleasure from it. They'd never noticed how time had passed in the earth realm, because on their excursions they had focused only on their over-powering hunger. Nothing else had existed.

"I want to go back," Macduff said and turned to face him.

"To Nefandus?" Samuel asked.

Macduff nodded.

"You can't. You know what they do to Renegades. They won't put you in the digs."

"I don't care. It's what I deserve," Macduff said miserably.

"You're going to surrender?" Samuel stood and started pacing, his fear turning to anger. "I can't believe you've lost your daring. You were always smarter and braver than me."

"That's not true." Macduff raised himself on one elbow.

"Sure it is," Samuel answered. "Even in Nefandus, you were the one who had the courage to meet the Dark Goddess. I never would have."

Macduff tossed the blankets away and swung his legs over the side of the bed. Samuel was surprised to see how much weight he had lost.

"I was a fool to do that," he said, his frustration matching Samuel's. "I know why they call her the death bringer now. I might as well be dead."

"You defended her," Samuel maintained. "You said it was only because she had been called upon when people were dying that she became a bad omen. You convinced me it was okay to pray to her for strength. You said—"

"I didn't tell you the truth," Macduff said quietly.

Samuel glared at him, waiting.

"She came to me, but not because I'd been praying to her," Macduff confessed. "It was always you she wanted."

"What do you mean *me*?" Samuel asked, knowing he wasn't going to like the answer.

"I was only a messenger," he said. "She wanted you to escape. She was hell-bent on getting you back to the earth realm before the autumnal equinox."

"Is she the one who told you about the portals?" Samuel asked, dismayed. "She gave you the pocket watches, didn't she? You didn't steal them like you said."

Macduff started to speak but stopped and

cocked his head, listening. Samuel heard it, too; the muted, stealthy voices. He eased to the door and touched the knob. Static electricity spiked from his finger. Silently he slipped the dead bolt into place.

"Regulators," Macduff whispered. He had a wild look.

Samuel pressed his ear against the door and listened to Ashley talking to someone in the next room. Alarm shot through him.

"We've got to go," Samuel said. "She's turning us over to Regulators."

But Macduff had crawled back under the covers.

"You're going with me," Samuel declared. "And then I guarantee we'll find a way to get normal again and return home."

"Go," Macduff urged. "I want them to capture me. I can't live this way anymore."

"You don't know what you're saying." Samuel wrapped his arms around Macduff. Even though Samuel could feel his friend's ribs and spine, Macduff was still a heavy weight to move. "I got you into this mess in the first place, so there's no way I'm leaving you behind now."

"You'll only get yourself captured if you try to take me," Macduff said, pushing Samuel away.

"You're my friend," Samuel answered, determined. "I won't go without you."

CHAPTER SEVEN

THE DOOR BROKE open, and two brawny men stumbled into the room, their black suits stretched tight across their massive shoulders. They stopped at an arm's length from Samuel.

The one with a knotty forehead worked his jaw as if he were trying to remember how to speak when disguised. His bumpy brow smoothed, and words tumbled from his mouth like stones.

"The master wants you back," he announced.

The second Regulator twitched, and a corona of sparks circled him. His thick legs dwindled into pointed elfin toes. He caught Samuel looking and immediately his feet reformed into round-toed green boots. His gray eyes hardened.

"They're new recruits," Samuel assessed. "We can outsmart them. I bet they've never even been in this world before."

"Are you crazy? Even novices have more power than we have. You go," Macduff whispered. "I'll stall them."

Samuel glanced at the window. "I've got a plan."

"I know what you're thinking and it won't work," Macduff argued. "They'll get you for sure. You can't change to shadow before they can."

"Are you daring me?" Samuel said, eager to try.

Macduff groaned, knowing his caution only goaded Samuel. "Don't," Macduff warned. "They want us to make a run for it. You know what they can do to us then."

"Stop." The first Regulator raised his hand stiffly. Two fingers had melded together into a lump. "The master is willing to take you back."

"What do you think?" Macduff asked. Even in the dim light Samuel could see hope firing in Macduff's eyes. "Should we go with them?"

"Think about it," Samuel countered. "What would the master want with us? Was our digging so fine that he needs us back for that?"

"Maybe it's on account of what you are," Macduff said. "It's a chance."

"You and I have got a lot more talking to do." Samuel placed his arms under Macduff's and hugged his chest tightly.

"Where do you get this courage?" Macduff asked.

"It's easy when you have no choice," Samuel countered.

The first Regulator trundled forward.

"I am not going to let them catch us," Samuel said and made his grip stronger.

"Don't," Macduff answered.

Samuel ignored him. "On the count of

three," he said. He could feel Macduff's heart thundering beneath his fingers

"Maybe their clumsiness is an act, because they want to—"

Samuel exploded into ebony grains, and the impact made Macduff's head snap back. He screamed. His chest elongated, and then he vanished with a loud *thwack*. His wraithlike shadow joined Samuel's murky apparition.

Outside, rain hit them, cold and sharp. Samuel charged straight up into the storm. Howling winds slapped their cobwebby forms and tossed them about.

Watch out! Macduff shouted mentally.

Too late. Samuel saw the large machine thumping downward. Its hard vibration drummed through them. The mechanism had no wings and was too squat to be an airplane, but the blade on top twirled like a propeller. As it continued to descend, it created an unnatural wind that jostled them, pushing them down to the pavement.

Samuel slithered to a walkway on a bridge and materialized. The river below was swollen with rainwater and debris, its turbulent roar drowning the noise from the traffic.

Macduff shivered and coughed. "It's a helicopter," he answered, before Samuel could even ask. Their friendship had always been that close: one answering the other's question before it had even been spoken.

Then Samuel sensed something else.

Macduff pointed to the lamppost. Translucent shadows swirled around the light. The bulb flickered, then exploded, and shards of glass cascaded into the rain.

"I told you we couldn't outrun them," Macduff said. His teeth chattered.

"The chase isn't over yet," Samuel said.

A black spectral cloud curled, then swooped down and thickened. Two bulky shapes forged, and the Regulators walked forward, disguised as two men. Vapors spewed behind them. Their faces, still black smudges, continued to take shape, noses and chins poking out.

Samuel hoped a driver might witness this supernatural display and stop to help, but no car even slowed. Frantic, Samuel looked over the railing. Whitecaps foamed and disappeared in whirlpools.

"That's our escape." Samuel threw one leg over the railing. "Once we get in the water it'll be hard for the Regulators to catch us. I bet they can't swim."

Macduff didn't move.

"We can still get away," Samuel said in an urgent tone and straddled the guardrail. "The current can't be any worse than the Ohio River when it overflowed its banks."

Macduff didn't respond.

"Don't give up," Samuel pleaded.

The Regulators lunged at them, hands whacking the air wildly.

In the same moment, a siren pierced the night. A black-and-white car pulled to the side of the road. A panel of blue lights flickered across its roof. Two men wearing uniforms and holstered guns jumped out.

"At last we got some help," Samuel said excitedly to Macduff.

But the two men ran past the Regulators and sprinted toward them. With a shock

Samuel realized they were trying to stop him from jumping.

"Now!" Samuel screamed. He grabbed on to Macduff and jumped. Macduff let out a gasp and they plummeted back, somersaulting into darkness.

Samuel hit the water first. The impact knocked the air from his lungs. The current was cold and swift. It tore around him and ripped Macduff from his arms. Samuel swam hard, trying to catch up to his friend. But Macduff had panicked. He flailed his arms as if he had forgotten how to swim. Samuel tried to rescue him, but something beneath the water's surface hit his side. He gasped for air and treaded water, turning, trying to find Macduff again. The cold had leeched his strength, and his movements were sluggish now. He cleared his throat, took a breath and dove, but the river was too strong. The current carried him away from the bridge.

"Macduff!" he shouted, but his voice had weakened, and he doubted anyone could hear his cry.

The river caught him again and swept him downstream. In one last futile effort he tried to dissolve into shadow and float away, but his body was too feeble and cold. He tucked into a ball, facing forward, and let the current take him. He drifted into unconsciousness, thinking about Macduff and home.

CHAPTER EIGHT

SOMETHING TAPPED the back of Samuel's head. He opened his eyes, disoriented, and tried to sit up. Freezing waters rushed over him and sprayed his face. Then he remembered he was in the river, but he was no longer moving with the current. He was entangled in an island of debris. He rested his cheek on slimy black leaves. Their rank, moldy smell filled his lungs. He had lost Macduff, and now he wanted to stay there and let his sorrow drown him.

The tapping started again, harder this time, rousing him from his stupor. He blinked. Large wings fanned over him, and in his semi-conscious state, he imagined a raven perched on a branch above him, its feathers slick and dripping rain. Samuel tried to grab a tailfeather, but the bird was quicker. It pecked his hand, drawing blood, and cackled.

"What do you want with me?" Samuel asked, coughing.

The bird let out a strident yell, then turned its head, eyeing him.

Fully conscious now, Samuel took a mental inventory. Except for the sore throat and numbness in his legs, he felt all right. His side still ached from whatever had hit him earlier, but no real damage had been done. He checked his pockets, frantic until his fingers found the watch. He hoped the water hadn't ruined it.

Samuel willed his body to release and transform into a shadow, but after several tries, he gave up and gripped a branch. He started to pull himself up, but the limb broke with a loud crack and splashed into the river, narrowly missing his eye.

The raven made a ticking sound as if

scolding him. Then it fluttered its wings, and a dreamy feeling came over Samuel. In the reverie, he saw himself flying with the bird. The raven screeched, and the painful cry awakened a hidden strength. Samuel concentrated. This time he became a black mist rising from the water. He was still too weak and cold to soar high into the night, but the bird seemed to understand and circled in low-flying loops as Samuel crept up the banks, a puny puff of fog. He followed the bird from the channel and continued low to the ground, undulating around shrubs and weeds, the dank smells of earth and rain melding into him.

After a few minutes his energy dissipated. His shadow dawdled, too heavy to float. He skimmed over puddles and bumped against the ground. He needed to find someplace safe to spend the night. He doubted it would take the Regulators long to find him at the pace he was going now.

Suddenly, the bird screamed in victory, as if Samuel had reached his destination, and it flew off, abandoning him at the entrance to a cemetery. The rows of gravestones stretched for as far as he could see. The sacred ground would offer protection.

Samuel materialized, certain no one was around. He pushed open the ornate iron gates of a small mausoleum. The gloom inside was uninviting, the musty smell worse, but both were better than staying outside in the downpour. He batted at the gluey cobwebs covering the entrance. A sudden creeping sensation made him stop and turn.

He wasn't alone.

CHAPTER NINE

SAMUEL STEPPED back into the rain. A girl walked toward him, carrying a beam of light. Her face, illuminated in the glow, looked angelic, and, for a moment, he thought she was an apparition. A wet cape clung to her shoulders, and the hood did little to protect her from the downpour. Her white-blond hair clung to her neck, and raindrops sparkled across her cheeks like a spray of diamonds.

"I knew you'd come," she said accusingly and focused the light on him.

He shielded his eyes against the glare. "How did everyone know I was coming through?"

"You have to return here," she answered simply.

"I do?"

"I read the lore. I know all about you." She let the shaft of light fall and, without the brightness blinding him, he noticed a silver object in her other hand that looked like a knife. He examined her more closely, wondering why she was there in the dead of night with a weapon.

"Don't stare at me," she commanded, and the light flashed back to his eyes in warning. "I'm not going to let you hypnotize me."

"Why would I do that?" he asked, trying to distract her while he took a quick step forward. He had intended to disarm her, but his legs wobbled, too numb from cold, and he stumbled back against the stone wall.

In the same moment she thrust the silver object at him. He grimaced, expecting to feel pain. Instead he stared, dumbfounded, at a crucifix held shakily two inches from his nose.

"You can't harm me," she said boldly, and, with the hand that held the light, she opened her cape to show him the thick, pointed stakes hanging from a rope tied around her waist. "I came prepared."

"For what?" he asked, dismayed.

She stepped back and clenched her jaw. "I bet you never thought anyone would figure out that you're a vampire."

Samuel knew about vampires. Mr. Paul, who had lived on a neighboring homestead, had been forced to leave his farm in central Europe when vampirism had made it too risky for him to stay. His stories had frightened Samuel, but Samuel's father had laughed and said his tales were only an old man's way of getting attention. Now Samuel wondered if the undead had become a problem in modern times. If so, Ashley hadn't mentioned it.

"I'm not a vampire," he said firmly.

"Right," the girl answered sarcastically and passed the light over his body. "You just dug yourself out of a grave."

He glanced down. He did look as if he'd just burrowed through six feet of earth. Silt and mud soiled his clothes, and rotting black leaves clung to him. Then, with a start he remembered he had been careless when he had materialized moments earlier.

"I saw you transform from mist," she added triumphantly.

Her bravery amazed him. If he had witnessed what she must have seen, he didn't think he would have had the courage to stay and face the supernatural.

"I won't hurt you," she said in a conciliatory voice, and slowly lowered her hand. "I promise I won't tell anyone what you are, but in return I want you to help me."

"What do you think I can do for you?"

"I want you to free Emily," she said.

"Free her from what?" he asked, not understanding what she expected him to do.

"She's my best friend." Her voice had taken on a threatening tone. "And I won't accept what is happening to her."

"What do I have to do with Emily?" None of this was making sense to Samuel.

"Look, Macduff—"

"Macduff? You think I'm Macduff?" At

least now he understood what had happened to Emily.

"She told me your name," the girl said coolly. "I know she's under your spell, or curse, or whatever you call it when you suck someone's blood."

"I'm not Macduff." His thoughts drifted, remembering the times they had been brought into the earth realm to hunt. How could he return someone's life force once it had been taken? Maybe there wasn't a way. The master had never told them how to reverse what they had done. "I wish I could help you, but . . ."

"But what?" she asked impatiently.

"Macduff wasn't a vampire," he said at last.

"Don't lie to me." She thrust the crucifix at him. The metal edge grazed his cheek, but this time he caught her wrist and twisted her arm. Her hood fell back, revealing beautiful, brooding eyes.

"Macduff loved Emily. He didn't mean to hurt her." Samuel pulled the girl closer, hoping she would see the sincerity in his expression, but when she was next to him, the air around her overflowed with the sweet fragrance of fear. Her bravado had only been an act to hide her terror. He admired her even more now.

"What did Macduff do to her?" She tried to pull free, but he tightened his hold, his cold fingers feeling the rapid pulse in her veins.

He swallowed hard, knowing he should leave; the scent of prey enveloped her now, and the pressure was building inside him.

"Tell me," she said in a small voice, her confidence gone.

The need awakened in him stronger than he had ever felt it before. It swept through him with a feverish ache. He caught her shoulders and drew her against his chest until he could experience her racing heartbeat; then he bent down and whispered against her ear. "Evil has many names, but I know its one true identity. Part of it lives in me."

She tried to pull away, but he didn't release her. She had stirred the predator inside him, and he relished her struggle.

"Another world exists in a dimension par-alleling earth's," he went on. "I come from there."

"Let me go," she said gruffly and tried to bite him.

He laughed at her futile attempt and clamped his hand over her mouth, her breath warm and enticing against his palm.

"Since ancient times, people have been lured into Nefandus." He eased his lips onto her temple, tasting the rain on her skin, and continued. "I was promised an elixir to cure my great-grandfather Elijah. Instead I was made a *servus*, a slave, and given powers. But with those gifts came a hunger; a need that can only be filled—" He tilted her head and gazed into her eyes, enjoying her stark terror, then he cupped his muddy hands around her small face. "Let me show you."

He placed his lips over hers, and drew breath from her lungs. He pulled deeper, slowly leeching her life force. With one sip his strength returned, making him ravenous for more. She sighed, and he knew he would take her.

But without warning her hand came up and jammed the crucifix into his cheek. He fell back, howling. Warm blood rushed through his fingers, and the predator inside him curled back behind his soul. He stared at her, confused.

Rage had replaced her fear.

"Big joke! You guys are so not funny!" she shouted, as if she knew others were hiding nearby. She flashed the light over the gravestones, desperately searching for someone. "Don't you have anything better to do than to torment me?"

Rain ran down Samuel's neck and back. He rubbed his arms against the chill and began to shiver.

She glared at him, then spun around and walked away, her long cloak dragging over the wet grass and the gathering autumn leaves. "How'd you do that transforming bit anyway?" she asked over her shoulder, but she didn't wait for an answer. "I'll bet Barry figured that one out. Mr. Special Effects, with all his science. I hate you guys!"

Samuel wondered if others might have seen him transform. He hurried to catch up to her. "Who's watching us?"

"Don't pretend you don't know," she warned. "You've had your fun. You scared me. You won. The game is over."

"Game?" he asked, dodging a granite marker.

"I can't believe my brother!" she continued, seeming now to enjoy her rampage. "Why am I always part of my brother's initiation for the new guys on the football team?" She shook her head. "Sledge knew I was coming here, but he went too far this time. Doesn't he understand how worried I am about Emily?"

"Sledge is your brother?" Samuel asked, remembering the guy hassling Ashley in the locker room earlier that day.

"Get real." She strode rapidly around the headstones toward a huge, rusted car parked in the drive. Rainbow letters spelled out *Chicks Rule* across the back window.

Samuel paused, sensing the approach of something foul. A powerful current curled through the rain and encircled him. Blue sparks crackled over the trees. Regulators were nearby, trying to locate him. Samuel knew he needed to get far away from there as quickly as he could. He glanced back at the girl.

She had already reached the car and opened the door. She slid inside.

"Wait," he yelled and caught the door before she could close it. "Do you want to get even with your brother?"

She bit the corner of her lip, as if debating something important. "How?"

"Take me with you, and I'll tell you on the way," he said, hoping he could think of something. He needed the speed of her car; his body was too weak to transform.

"Is this part of it?" she asked.

"What?"

"Your initiation?"

He held up his hand as if taking an oath. "I swear it's not."

"I guess we could go to Nikki's party," she said, considering a plan of her own. "Sledge hates it when I pal around with his friends.

He'd die if I dated someone on the football team."

Samuel ran around to the other side of the car and got in before she could change her mind.

"You can't go to a party the way you are now." She looked him over. "Do you want to go to your house first?"

"I'll shower at your place and borrow some of Sledge's clothes," he said, eager to get moving.

A wry smile crossed her face and she turned the key. "That's perfect. He can't stand to have anyone wear his clothes." The engine rumbled but she didn't drive away.

"What's wrong?" he asked nervously, sensing the Regulators coming closer.

"Promise this isn't another joke," she said and her eyes held a plea that he couldn't refuse.

"I promise," he answered.

She smiled thinly, unconvinced, and jammed her foot on the gas pedal. The car sped forward. Rain hit the front window, and, as they passed through the cemetery gates, Samuel studied the roiling storm shadows. When he felt sure they were safe, he turned back to the girl.

"What's your name?" he asked finally.

"Like you don't know that," she said huffily, but then she reconsidered. "You probably don't. All my brother's friends call me Sister Sledge." She let out a heavy sigh and glanced at him. "Some of the more obnoxious ones even start singing 'We Are Family' when they see me."

"I'm Samuel." The joke was lost on Samuel, but he smiled anyway.

"I'm Madison Sledgeheimer," she answered after a careful pause. "Call me Maddie."

"I'm sorry about Emily."

Maddie tightened her hold on the steering wheel. "Emily is wasting away just like Lucy Westenra."

"Another friend?" Samuel asked. Macduff hadn't told him there were others.

"Dracula's victim in Bram Stoker's book," she answered, as if he should have known. "Nobody believes me, but why else would

Macduff have taken Emily to the cemetery?"

Samuel shrugged but he understood. Macduff had probably taken her there to escape Regulators.

"The groundskeeper found her, stumbling around the tombstones, disoriented and dazed. They thought she was a druggie at first. But as soon as her mother told me how they'd found her I knew what had really happened."

"But I bet she didn't have marks on her neck," Samuel said, trying to dismantle Maddie's theory.

"With all the technology we have today vampires have probably figured out a way to drain blood without leaving puncture wounds," Maddie countered. "I bet they file their canines until they're as sharp as hypodermic needles. Don't tell me they haven't found a way."

"I guess," Samuel said, his thoughts turning back to Macduff. He hoped his friend had escaped the river, but a dismal feeling shrouded him and he doubted he would ever see him again.

"It doesn't matter if you agree with me or

not," Maddie went on. "I'm going to save her."

"My mother was as headstrong as you are," Samuel said, remembering his mother's determination. "You would have made a fine pioneer."

She glanced at him to see if he was joking. When she saw his earnestness, she smiled appreciatively. "Thanks. I should have been born in another time. I know that."

"You'd want to live back then?" he asked.

"Absolutely," she answered with enthusiasm. "Wouldn't you?"

"Maybe." He shrugged and settled down into the seat, trying to get warm.

"I'll turn on the heater," she said brightly.

But the blast of air didn't help. His chill was soul-deep. He wondered what would have happened if Maddie's anger hadn't broken his trance. Would he have found the strength within himself to stop? He didn't know. He only knew he liked Maddie, and that meant he had to stay away from her.

CHAPTER TEN

MADDIE UNTIED HER wet cloak and flung it over a white chair. She plopped down on the edge of her bed, bouncing twice before she settled on the ruffled spread.

Samuel waited in the doorway.

"Don't worry about tracking dirt." She pulled off a mud-spattered boot and let it fall. It landed with a dull thump. "I'll tell my mom Sledge did it."

Samuel entered her room tentatively, his toes digging into the plush pink carpeting. White bookcases lined the walls. The shelves were filled with books on witches, vampires, spirits, and ghosts.

"I know what you're thinking." She stood and walked toward him. His muddy handprints still smudged her chin and cheeks.

"What am I thinking?" he asked, taking a cautious step away from her.

"You're wondering how I sleep at night." She pointed to the framed black-and-white pictures of vampires hanging above her bed. "Everyone gets the creeps from the Bela Lugosi photo, but I like it. My favorite is still the *Dark Shadows* print. I love Barnabas Collins."

Samuel stared at the sharp white fangs protruding over the man's lips. "What gave you such an interest—"

"In the occult?" she asked crisply. "My mom asks the same question every day." She stepped around him, leading him to another room across the hallway. "I saw a ghost when I was little. No one believes that either."

In the next room Samuel followed Maddie at a safe distance, stepping over shirts, jeans, and underwear piled on the floor. A poster-size picture of Sledge dressed in his football uniform decorated the wall above an unmade bed. Framed newspaper clippings and awards, all with Sledge's name, hung crookedly above a desk cluttered with empty water bottles.

Maddie flicked on a light in the bathroom and looked back at him. "Why are you acting so nervous? My mom isn't home and even if she did catch us upstairs, she'd just think you were one of Sledge's friends and I was helping you."

"Don't you have a boyfriend?" He stepped over to the bathtub. The smell of mildew and soap fought for dominance in the tiled room. Wet towels formed a mound in the corner.

She ignored his question and slid a mirrored panel aside. Bottles, tubes, razors, and brushes crammed the shelves. "You can use his stuff to shave. But I'd stay away from his cologne. It reeks."

Samuel nodded and peeled off his shirt.

"He's going to be so furious." She smiled conspiratorially. "I'll pick out some of his clothes and leave them on the bed for you."

When she had closed the door, Samuel removed Macduff's pocket watch, and carefully cleaned the case and crystal. He clicked it open and stared down at the miniature night sky enclosed in the golden circle. The water hadn't damaged its magic.

He turned on the shower and let the steam rise while he finished undressing, then he stepped into the tub. The spray washed over him, making the cut on his cheek sting. He tried to clear his mind. What had happened earlier with Maddie had frightened him and shown him his true potential. Remembering what he had done made a chill pass through him in spite of the hot water rushing down his back. He imagined an existence in which he was guided solely by his hunger, consuming relentlessly, no better than a vampire.

Macduff was right. He had no way to go back to his home on the frontier, and it was too dangerous for him to return to the digs in Nefandus. That left him stranded in a world in which he didn't belong and never would. He had to find a way to cope, the same way the pioneers had to figure out ways to survive in the wilderness.

But right now he had a more immediate problem. He needed to get away from Maddie before she triggered the predator inside him again, and he had to do it without making her suspicious. He couldn't just disappear.

Finally he turned off the water, dried himself with a towel, and dressed in the clothes left on the bed. Then he waited for Maddie in the hallway, pacing. The shoes she had given him felt heavy on his feet. His toes throbbed, and in spite of the calluses on his soles, he felt blisters forming.

When Maddie stepped out from her room, her eyes widened in surprise. "I can't believe the change," she said. "You look—"

She bit her lip as if embarrassed by what she had almost said, but her blush made him like her even more, and that only complicated his problem; he didn't want to hurt her feelings when he did leave.

"You look really pretty," he said, and he meant it.

Her silky hair touched her shoulders and covered more skin than the slash of cherry-colored skirt that hung below her hip bones. The wispy lace hem dangled jaggedly over her thighs.

Maddie cleared her throat, as if she weren't used to hearing compliments, and jingled her keys nervously.

"Come on," she said, walking stiffly down the stairs, obviously aware that he was watching her.

When they neared her car, she finally looked back at him. "Are you still watching me?" she asked, her cheeks crimson and speckled with raindrops.

"I would have thought you'd be used to guys staring at you," he countered.

"I'm Sledge's sister," she answered drily, as if that should have explained why guys didn't look at her.

"Your brother couldn't keep me away from you," Samuel said honestly.

She cast her eyes down and concentrated on unlocking the car door.

When they were buckled into their seatbelts, she started the car. The engine rumbled.

She turned a knob, and music filled the interior; then she steered away from the curb, singing loudly, her voice sweet and high.

A few minutes later, she parked under a tall palm tree. The rain was heavier now, coming down in sheets.

"Ready?" she asked, looking out at the storm.

They climbed from the car, and ran toward the corner house, laughing and splashing through puddles, their heads bent in the downpour.

Kids crowded the porch, some dancing, others drinking from bottles wrapped in brown paper bags. The music inside pounded, and Samuel liked the beat vibrating in the air.

Maddie pushed through the throng of guys smoking near the entrance. Samuel followed her into the overheated living room. Girls wore short skirts and clinging tops, their long legs shimmering with glitter. They pressed against the guys they were dancing with and swayed seductively.

"You're acting like you've never been to a party before." Maddie grabbed his hand and led him deeper into the mix. She smiled too brilliantly, and he had a feeling she was eager to show him off to her brother.

He surveyed the room. If Sledge and his friends were at the party, they weren't on the dance floor.

"Girls are so drooling over you," Maddie said, pulling his attention back to her. She gave him a tantalizing grin. "Dance with me."

He nodded and tried to remember the steps Ashley had taught him, but he could barely move his feet. The shoes pinched his toes. He'd never adjust to wearing anything but moccasins. He slipped out of the shoes and bent to pick them up, but a guy dancing between two girls accidentally kicked them aside. Samuel ducked and tried to retrieve them, but more feet were in the way.

Maddie stopped him. "Leave them," she said. "Sledge won't even miss them. He's got like a million pairs."

Samuel nodded and quickly forgot the shoes. It had been a long time since he'd been able to dance, and the rhythm was contagious.

His mind drifted back to the dancers of his own time, clapping and stomping their feet as the fiddler played. He had known all the steps and danced easily under the direction of a caller. But he knew better than to let out a whoop and swing Maddie around here.

"You're a little dance-impaired, aren't you?" Maddie wrapped her arms around his neck, her body close.

Carefully, he raised his hands and held her waist. Her bare hips moved beneath his fingers, her skin soft and comforting. But her closeness awakened other urges.

"Damn," he whispered and drew back, watching her.

Slowly Maddie slid her hands up her body, unembarrassed now by the way he was staring at her. She watched him watch her.

When the music stopped, she nuzzled his neck. He breathed the peachy fragrance of her white-blond hair. Memories came flooding back to him, ones he tried hard not to remember, of crimes the master had forced him to commit on the hunts, deeds that had left him inconsolable.

If he stayed, Maddie's fate would be the same as the other victims'. He had to leave her.

She brushed her hair from her forehead, then looked up at him. "Are you crying?"

"My eyes are tired," he lied.

Her tender look made him want to confide every horrible detail of his past to her, but instead he lied again. "I'm fine."

"We don't have to stay. Maybe playing around at the cemetery in all that rain gave you a fever."

She didn't wait for him to decide. She yanked his shirttail and led him toward the door.

"Hi, Samuel." Suddenly Ashley appeared, blocking his way. She cocked her head in a flirty way and wrapped her arms around him. "I didn't think you'd be able to come to Nikki's party."

"I imagine not," Samuel answered angrily, trying to free himself from her embrace.

Maddie looked quizzically from Samuel to Ashley. Her eyes locked on Ashley's finger, hooked possessively in Samuel's belt loop.

"Hi, Maddie," Ashley said sweetly. "I guess you've met my guy. Isn't he a hottie?"

"Your guy?" Maddie asked.

"No," Samuel started to explain, but Ashley was quicker.

"Sammy and I have been going together for months now," Ashley continued slyly and kissed his cheek.

"Whatever." Maddie turned sharply and shoved through the crowd, elbowing kids out of her way.

Samuel had been trying to come up with a reason to leave Maddie, but now that she had left him, he felt as if a mule had kicked him in the stomach.

"Maddie!" He tore away from Ashley and pushed his way through the dancers, trying to catch up to Maddie. When he finally burst outside into the cold rain, she had already reached her car.

He sprinted across the wet grass, calling to her, then jumped over a hedge as her car pulled away from the curb. He dodged into the street and ran around to the driver's side window.

"Maddie." He slapped his palm against the rain-slick glass.

"I can't believe you didn't tell me you were going with someone," she yelled back, her voice muffled. "You should have!"

The car lurched forward. He increased his pace and grabbed hold of the roof.

"I swear, Maddie. Ashley was just teaching me . . ." His words fell away. How could he say that she had been showing him how to flush a toilet and turn a spigot?

"I can just imagine what kind of lessons she was giving you," Maddie answered. "Everyone knows about Ashley."

The car accelerated and sped away. Samuel stood in the middle of the street, catching his breath, and looked at the taillights reflected in long red ribbons on the drenched pavement.

"It's for the best." Ashley walked toward him, twirling a large black umbrella, unmindful of the deep puddles through which her boots were sloshing.

"Stay away from me, Ashley," Samuel warned between gasps.

She ignored his request and stepped closer. "It's better if you let her go." She reached out and ran a finger over the scratch on his cheek as if she understood what had caused it. "You know what you would do to her eventually, but you don't have to worry about that with me."

"You're a bounty hunter." He glared at her. "And if something's happened to Macduff—"

"I didn't turn the two of you in," she argued back. "Besides, Macduff got away."

"How do you know?" He folded his arms over his chest and waited, trying not to let his hope rise. Ashley was duplicitous and he didn't want to be taken in by her again.

"He's still listed as a Renegade," she said simply and eased closer, offering him the shelter of her umbrella.

He turned away from her and started walking down the middle of the empty street. Rain pelted him.

"Do you really think I turned you over to Regulators?" she asked, hurrying behind him.

When he didn't turn back, she answered her own question. "If I had been planning to turn you in for a bounty, would I have bothered to show you how to use a microwave or turn on a TV?"

He ignored her.

"Maybe Berto's the one who told the Regulators you were with me. He's jealous of the way I feel about you," she explained.

Samuel stopped. "I don't think you could ever have real feelings for anyone."

"But I do." Her face softened with such a look of care that he almost believed she was concerned about him.

"Why me, then?" he asked. "I'm just a *servus* from the digs."

"You and I are the same," she said.

"I'm nothing like you," he answered.

"You want to go home, and that's all I want," she said. "I'll do anything to return to my own time, and I promise I'll help you get back to yours."

"What do I have to do?"

"Nothing."

"Nothing?" Samuel asked. "There's always a price to pay."

"I don't want anything from you," she said. "You can trust me."

"As far as I can trust the devil," Samuel answered bleakly.

He had had enough of this world. He started running with a slow, short stride. Soon his legs were taking long, smooth leaps, his arms pumping at his sides, his pace swift. Rain hit his face and curled coldly down his neck and chest, but the chill didn't steal his strength this time. He felt new resolve and hope. He was going to find Macduff, and then together they would figure out what to do for eternity.

His thoughts turned back to Ashley. Intuitively, he knew not to trust her, but what she had said made sense. She wouldn't waste time teaching him so many things if she planned to turn him over to Regulators for a reward. She had listened patiently, answered his questions, helped him with new words, and even tried to show him how to dance.

As he tried to figure out what Ashley wanted from him, he caught sudden movement in the corner of his eye. Fear shot through him.

He changed direction, but when he did, a flurry of golden letters spun from the dark. The ancient markings wove together, forging a shimmering net. Before he could run, the web had completely enveloped him. He struggled to free his arms, but instead he tripped and his forehead smacked the bumper of a parked car. He rolled facedown into a puddle, slipping into unconsciousness.

CHAPTER ELEVEN

THE SICKLY SWEET smell of burning roses made bile rise in Samuel's throat. He swallowed hard, trying to quell his uneasy stomach, but the movement only awakened the dull ache in his skull. Slowly he became aware of scuffling footsteps. Someone was walking around him. An instinctive caution took hold, the way it had in the wilderness when he had sensed danger before his mind could decipher the threat.

"He's awake," a familiar voice said. "Who's going to tell him?"

Samuel opened his eyes. Obie crouched beside him. Kyle stood above him, silhouetted against a tall window that looked out at the night. The rain had stopped, and the sky was clear. A fire burned nearby in a brick hearth. Logs crackled, and shot sparks up the chimney.

"Tell me what?" Samuel asked.

"I'm sorry I had to use magic on you," Obie said. "But we needed to talk to you. You weren't supposed to hit your head on a car."

"Magic?" Samuel asked. He tried to move, but the mysterious lettering still held him, flowing over him in unending patterns, weaving a delicate tapestry that bound him tightly.

Obie waved his hand and the streaming letters dissolved into glittering dust.

"You cast a spell on me?" Samuel asked, stating the obvious, and sat up.

"It was the only way to catch you," Berto said, walking toward him. He had been gazing at a huge painting of a forest in Nefandus as if he were homesick.

Samuel touched the knot on his forehead. "Can you use your magic to get rid of the pain?"

Obie smiled and waggled his index finger, writing something in the air.

Immediately, the bump on Samuel's head vanished, along with the throbbing.

"Truce?" Obie extended his hand. An inscription was tattooed on his wrist, consisting of the same mysterious symbols that had tethered Samuel.

"What was so all-fired important that you had to kidnap me?" Samuel asked, refusing to take the outstretched hand

"Time is running out," Berto said. "Together we have to fulfill the Legend."

"You're talking about the Legend of the Four again?" Samuel asked, and looked from one to the other. They were probably Sons of the Dark. Every *servus* had heard of the Renegades who had sworn their allegiance to the Goddess of the Dark Moon, but Samuel had always envisioned the Sons to be more powerful—paranormal warriors, like messengers from God, with spreading wings and imposing statures—and now these three ordinary-looking fellows were claiming to be the ones who would free the *servi* and seal the entrance to Nefandus so that others could no longer be abducted and enslaved there.

"You still think I'm the fourth?" Samuel surveyed the room, looking for a way to escape.

"Some of us do." Obie looked at Kyle.

"I'm not even convinced we're three of the Four," Kyle shot back. He didn't seem to take pride in the fact that he might be legendary. He acted as if a terrible burden had descended upon him. "And if we are, then I'm still not convinced that he's part of it."

"We think your destiny is to be with us when we go back to Nefandus—" Berto started.

"No." Samuel held up his hands as if pushing the idea away. "I'm definitely not going back there, and you're deluding yourselves if you think you can go back and free even one *servus*."

"I go back to Nefandus all the time," Kyle said.

"Sneaking back inside is one thing, but have you ever been to the digs?" Samuel asked, his mind racing back to the discarded *servi* who lived in the dump. "Even if you did free them, then what? Do you think they would fit into this world?"

Berto and Obie glanced at each other, as if Samuel were stating something they had considered.

"We have to fulfill the Legend," Obie cautioned. "If they are meant to be freed then we'll be shown a way to take care of them. We have to do it. It's the only way we'll be able to return to our own times and live out a normal life."

"So it's for selfish reasons that you're doing this," Samuel countered, and then he paused. It suddenly occurred to him that they might each have been reared in a different era before they were kidnapped and taken into Nefandus. He hadn't considered before that they could be like him, stranded in a time in which they didn't belong. "What time period do you call home?"

"I'm from here," Kyle countered, as if he didn't want to be included with the others.

"I'm the barbarian," Obie said proudly. "I'm trapped sixteen hundred years from my home."

"Toltec nation," Berto added. "I belong to one of the world's greatest civilizations."

"I come from the frontier along the Ohio River," Samuel said, suddenly feeling as if they were his friends. "My home's two hundred years away."

"You've had your reunion," Kyle said impatiently. "Now back to business."

"We don't know everything yet," Berto said. "That's the problem. We only know that we need to join together before the autumnal equinox."

"We're not sure you're the one," Kyle put in. "There's still enough time for someone else to come through."

"How do you know it has something to do with the autumnal equinox?" Samuel asked, but his thoughts remained focused on Kyle, wondering why he was so against him.

Berto hesitated, and when he finally spoke, he looked as if he were watching a memory. "Tezcatlipoca helps me sometimes."

"Start from the beginning," Obie said, and then to Samuel he added, "Berto can project his consciousness astrally, outside his body."

"You're a dream walker?" Samuel asked.

He was familiar with the concept. His great-grandfather had been captured by the Shawnee when he was a boy and adopted into a family. He had told Samuel that the shamans walked through dreams in order to heal people.

Berto smiled. "Sometimes when I'm inside my dreams, I visit with Tezcatlipoca. He carries a mirror that has magical qualities and gives clairvoyance to anyone who is allowed to gaze on it. The great lord took me back to Tenochtitlan and showed me his dark sun, the obsidian mirror. The smoke cleared, and when it did, I knew that the Four must come together before the day when the sun crosses the equator from the northern to the southern hemisphere."

"But did you see the face of the fourth one?" Kyle interrupted. "Maybe it's just a coincidence that Samuel came through now. Does he have a power?"

"None, other than the ones the master gave me," Samuel answered. "I'm as ordinary as the day is long."

"What are you talking about, Kyle?" Obie blurted out. "You don't have a special power either, only those of a slave, and yet you're one of the Four. Why are you being so skeptical? I thought we'd settled all of this before."

"I'd just like proof. Ashley's trouble, and he's been hanging out with her," Kyle said, but his suspicion of Samuel seemed to go deeper than that. "I don't see how we can trust him yet."

"I guess that's a roundabout way of saying you don't trust me," Berto said, clenching his hands.

"Okay," Kyle conceded. "I fell for her, too. Who wouldn't?"

"And your point is?" Bert asked defensively.

"It's so obvious she's using Samuel. He probably doesn't even know what she's doing with him." Kyle's tone implied that Samuel was a simpleton.

"I think she's just like us," Samuel said. The others turned to stare at him as if they had forgotten he was there. "She's trying to figure out a way to survive here."

"Samuel's right," Berto agreed. "She

wants to go home and she's chosen the only way she could find. She knows when she turns in Renegades she'll receive an increase in her time-traveling power. She'll keep doing that until she can go home someday."

Obie nodded. "You can't understand that, Kyle, because this is your time, and you like living in L.A., but when I first arrived I would have done anything to go back to my own time."

Kyle glared at him. "Maybe you should ask Ashley to tell you her real name and then look her up in the history books. Why does she even want to go back?"

Berto turned to Kyle, obviously frustrated. "Why won't you tell us what you know?"

"Would you believe me?" Kyle asked and then quickly answered his own question. "You're too in love with her to accept the truth."

"Maybe she figures she can change things if she does go back," Samuel put in and knew immediately his answer had irritated Kyle.

"It's almost morning." Obie interrupted,

as if he were trying to stop the escalating tension. "Let's get some sleep."

"We don't want to force you to stay," Berto said to Samuel. "We really are trying to keep you safe."

"And we were hoping you'd know something about the Legend," Obie said. "The rest of us have heard bits and pieces. Maybe you have something to add to the puzzle."

Samuel shook his head.

"Follow me." Kyle started across the large room filled with easels holding canvases. "I'll show you where you can sleep."

Samuel trailed Kyle down a hallway, then stepped through a doorway into a smaller room with windows that stretched from the ceiling to the floor.

"Berto and Obie are excited about having you join us," Kyle said. "But I have my doubts."

"You don't need to tell me that," Berto said. "Any fool can see you don't like me."

"It's not personal," Kyle explained. "I'm just cautious. Maybe Tezcatlipoca can see into the future, but Berto's god also has a reputation for being sinister and untrustworthy. He's known as a dark and most merciless deity. So how can we be so sure that you've come to help us and not destroy us?"

Samuel nodded, understanding Kyle now. He was like some of the frontiersmen who didn't trust anyone, because survival meant they had to be suspicious of everyone, even their friends.

"Why did you choose to escape now?" Kyle went on and planted himself firmly in the doorway.

"I don't think I should waste my time answering questions from someone who's not going to believe what I have to say anyway," Samuel said coldly. Distrust worked two ways.

But surprisingly, his response seemed to satisfy Kyle. He nodded and walked away.

Samuel stretched out on the bed in the corner and waited until the soft rhythms in the house had settled; then he crept to his doorway, determined to do a little investigating of his own, but when he tried to push through the entrance a film held him back. He pressed against it with the flat of his palm. Rushing across his skin were tiny marks as fine as the threads on a spiderweb. Obie's magic letters had sealed his exit. Despite what they had said, they had imprisoned him. They didn't trust him any more than he trusted them.

CHAPTER TWELVE

KYLE SPIT INTO the kitchen sink and then turned back to Samuel, who was still eating at the table with Berto and Obie. "What were you thinking?" he asked, and wiped his lips with a paper towel.

"My mom made good squirrel and dumplings," Samuel said in defense of his cooking. "I didn't do anything she didn't do. The squirrels were a little scrawny, so I added some pork fat to the broth, and the greens were hard to find. I only picked a few—"

"When I said it was your turn to make dinner, I meant for you to take money and go to the grocery store." Kyle ripped open a bag of chocolate cookies and tossed one into his mouth.

"The squirrel tastes good." Obie picked up a bone and sucked on it.

Kyle opened the refrigerator and looked inside. "You didn't even buy milk."

"I couldn't find a cow," Samuel lied. He had been so excited to show off his cooking that he'd forgotten to go to the store and buy the food on the list, but if Kyle wanted to believe he was a country bumpkin, then he would play the part.

Samuel turned back to his meal and took a huge bite, relishing the gamey flavor. He'd been living with Kyle, Obie, and Samuel for almost a week now, and even though they were friendly enough, they remained aloof, and his visit felt strained. He had sensed that they were always watching him, so he had been surprised when two days earlier Kyle had told him it would be all right for him to go out on his own.

Now Kyle frowned as if another trouble-some thought were nagging at him. "Where did you skin the squirrels?"

"In the park," Samuel answered, wishing

Kyle would stop pestering him so he could finish his dinner. It was the first good meal he'd had since leaving home. "I didn't soil your precious floors, if that's what you're worried about."

"And the skins?"

"I hung them over a tree branch. I'll get them later."

Kyle slammed his fist down on the counter. "I give up."

"What now?" Samuel pushed his plate away. "You told me it was my turn to fix dinner and I did."

"You don't understand." Kyle raked both hands through his hair. "In your time skinning a squirrel was common, but here authorities will find the pelts and think some sicko is torturing squirrels before he moves up the scale to humans."

"When you tell me a rule, I follow it." Samuel stared defiantly at him. "Even when your rules don't make sense I go along with what you tell me, but you never once told me about any laws against hunting squirrel."

"We always buy our food at grocery stores," Kyle said with rising frustration. "Haven't you taken in anything?"

"You've done more than your share of preaching," Samuel answered, his throat tightening with anger. "This isn't an easy place to figure out and—"

"It's my fault," Berto put in and spooned more gravy onto his biscuit. "Samuel said he wanted to hunt something for dinner to surprise you, and I took him up to Griffith Park. I wasn't thinking. I thought it would be funny to feed you squirrel."

"It was," Obie said, obviously trying to control his laughter. "I thought you were going to vomit."

Kyle shook his head. "You guys have to be more careful."

"Relax." Berto grinned. "You worry too much about the authorities."

"Besides, you liked the squirrel meat before you knew what it was," Obie added, giving Samuel a mischievous wink.

Kyle tried to smile. He swung his leg over

his chair and sat down. "If you tell me it tastes like chicken I'll pound you."

Obie grinned.

Samuel picked at his dumpling, pushing it around his plate. He didn't understand the way the others could tuck away their hard feelings so quickly. He still felt annoyed with Kyle. Then he understood: they were as tight as three brothers, and he was the outsider.

"After dinner, we'll talk some more," Kyle said, trying to be friendly, but his voice had taken on the patronizing tone that Samuel had come to detest.

Samuel pushed back his chair, ignoring their surprised looks.

"I'm going for a run." He fled through the door and didn't wait for the elevator. Instead he took the stairs, leaping down the last five steps of each flight to the next landing.

Outside, his feet smacked the concrete with a hard sound. He angled through the labyrinth of shoppers jamming the sidewalk. During the past week Kyle had spent every afternoon showing Samuel around Los Angeles and telling him how to participate and mingle, as if he were too rustic to possess even the most ordinary social skills. Come Monday, Kyle expected him to start school, but Samuel didn't see much sense in the plan. He wanted to go back to his own time, and schooling wasn't going to help with that.

On the next block he caught his reflection in a barbershop window and stopped. He looked as if he fit in. His clothes were right and so was the new haircut, but he felt separate from the crowd pushing around him. He had known who he was on the frontier. Pioneers envied his reckless bravery. He had even developed an identity in Nefandus—someone the other *servi* depended on—but who was he in this time?

Barely perceptible images in the corner of the window made him lean forward. He brushed away the grime with his shirtsleeve. Tiny, runic letters hovered behind him like a swarm of gnats, almost invisible but for the sunlight glinting across their constantly moving forms. He had thought the others trusted him.

Now he saw the real reason Kyle had let him leave the apartment on his own: Obie's magic chaperoned him. Just as quickly, another thought needled him. Maybe the incantation was a spell to spy on him.

He started walking again, brushing through the crowd. He stared longingly at the happy families standing in long lines in front of the restaurants. He was never going to fit into this bleak world of buildings, pavement, and car exhaust. His chest seemed to collapse under the burden of his loneliness, and his heart filled with an inconsolable longing to see his parents, brothers, sisters, and great-grandfather. Maybe if Macduff were with him the problems wouldn't seem so insurmountable, but right now he'd do anything to go home.

Anything? A voice whispered across his mind.

He turned, and the guardian runes buzzed nervously. Then, sweeping closer, the letters formed a different incantation and remained, like a crown, above his head.

"Nice haircut." Ashley walked toward him,

her green dress clinging to her hips. She looked him up and down, then stepped closer and pinched his spiky hair. Her sweet perfume enveloped them. "You look as if you're adjusting well. Most Renegades aren't as lucky as you. They end up wandering the streets, dazed and begging for food."

"You say that like you know from firsthand experience," he answered.

"Maybe." She smoothed her palm over his cheek, then tilted her head, coaxing. "You didn't answer my question."

"Which was?"

"Would you really do anything to go home?"

"Who wouldn't?" he asked glumly.

"Let me take you back to your own time."

His heart beat wildly. Was it possible to travel that far into the past?

The runic symbols around him bound together, weaving into a rope, and started circling around him.

Ashley batted the intertwined letters away. The magic shattered in a spray of golden dust.

The specks crusted the sidewalk, then fluttered and twitched, trying to take form again. Ashley ground them into the concrete with her pointy-toed shoe.

"Obie's spell-casting isn't strong enough to resist me yet," she said wryly and offered her hand to Samuel again.

"Take me home," he whispered hoarsely. He clasped her fingers and braced himself, knowing there would be a terrible price to pay.

CHAPTER THIRTEEN

A REVOLVING BLACK disk appeared behind Ashley. As it rotated, it grew, the gravitational pull becoming stronger as the circle increased in size. Samuel felt drawn toward the center. His feet slipped and he struggled against its force. Old newspapers, gum wrappers, and cigarette butts whirled past him, spinning into the hole.

Some of the spectators who had gathered on the sidewalk to watch the mysterious circle suddenly stepped back, afraid, while others came closer for a better look.

"People are watching us." Samuel became concerned for the safety of the growing number assembling around them.

"Don't worry," Ashley encouraged. "In a few minutes none of them will have even been born."

A sudden sharp tug sucked him into the tunnel as brilliant white light exploded around him. Ashley still held his hand, and together they plummeted downward. Just when he had gotten used to the pace, the velocity increased. He shrieked, and the scream used his last breath. Tiny flecks like particles of sand bombarded him, stinging his skin.

A dim, greenish light cast bewitching shadows across Ashley's face. She watched him, visibly enjoying his fear and shock. He had made a terrible mistake. He realized that now. No wonder the others had been so worried about him. They must have sensed how naive and vulnerable he was.

The pressure became unbearable, but the force didn't appear to bother Ashley. She concentrated on her wristwatch. The face, like the one Macduff had given Samuel, displayed a rapidly changing night sky.

Suddenly, the downward rush slowed. Samuel inhaled the fuzzy air, and his lungs, starved for oxygen, burned with the first poisonous breath.

Ashley glanced up at him.

"I can tell the year and season by the position of the stars." In the effervescing air, her words wobbled. "But I'm looking for an exact day, and that's more difficult."

"Why don't you go back home to your own time?" Samuel asked.

"I don't have the power yet," she answered. "But I will soon."

Suddenly, stark white light slit the dark in front of them.

"We've arrived," Ashley shouted, releasing him.

Samuel tumbled away from her and fell through the opening. His jaw hit something solid, and pain shot down his spine. Then he skidded across hard-packed earth, scraping his palms. Sunlight flashed in his eyes. He came to a stop, his cheek resting on a stone, and lay sprawled on his stomach. He took in one long draw of clean fresh air and with that first breath caught the rich smells of his mother's crackling bread.

He lifted his head. He had landed in the clearing around his parents' cabin.

"Mother!" he shouted, but no one rushed outside to greet him.

Ashley stepped out of the churning black disk, and, when she did, it vanished. The tree branches rustled in its wake.

"Is this real?" Samuel asked, afraid that it was only an illusion.

"Go inside and see." She sauntered toward him. "I'll wait for you here."

He scrambled to his feet. "No need for you to stay," he yelled. "I'm not going back with you."

"I'll just hang out for a while then," she said and lifted her face to the sun. "And gather up some rays."

"Suit yourself." He ran into the cabin. The homey smells of wood smoke and cornbread hung in the air.

"Mother!" he called again, and turned about, his eyes adjusting rapidly to the muted light. Lunch was set out on the rough-hewn table, untouched, waiting for his family to eat. "Where is everyone?"

He grabbed a piece of crackling bread, his mouth watering with anticipation. He jammed it into his mouth, relishing the salty taste of rendered salt pork. Then he touched the pot of beans. The kettle felt cool. Why would his mother have set out lunch only to have his family abandon it?

"Sam," a familiar voice came from the corner beneath the loft where his younger brothers slept.

"Grandpa?"

His great-grandfather Elijah sat in the rocking chair, quilts wrapped about his shoulders and draped over his lap. He had spent many days throughout his long illness sitting in the same place.

"Where is everyone?" Samuel stepped into the cool darkness, but as he drew closer, the change in Elijah's appearance startled him.

The old man had carefully painted red lines across his wrinkled face and had plucked his hair, leaving only a tuft on the top of his head, as he had told Samuel he had worn it when he lived with the Shawnee. His scalp lock was decorated with three eagle feathers.

"What are you doing dressed like that?" Samuel asked.

"Waiting for you," Elijah answered.

The Shawnee sometimes adopted a captured enemy, believing that after a cleansing ritual, the prisoner would assume the identity of a deceased relative. In his youth Elijah had gone through such a purification ceremony, replacing the lost son of a powerful shaman.

At times like this, Samuel believed that Elijah had become the shaman's dead son. Before returning to the pioneer's world, he had learned how to call forth spirit animals. Some settlers even claimed that they had seen him transform into a mountain lion and fly over the treetops, but Samuel figured too much whiskey had helped them see the flying feline.

"You have a new wound." His great-grandfather spoke quietly, his feeble voice pulling Samuel away from his thoughts. "But the cut looks as if it has been healing for a week, and yet you've only been gone a few hours," Elijah continued. His cold, knobby fingers rubbed Samuel's cheek where Maddie had dug the crucifix into his skin. "You didn't have this deep scratch when you waved good-bye to me this morning."

Then he looked down at Samuel's feet and nodded knowingly. "And when I saw you last, you were wearing moccasins. A few hours later you come back to me wearing strange and foreign clothing, your hair cut short."

A chill raced through Samuel. Ashley had brought him back to the very day he had set out with Macduff to find the trapper's campsite and get the elixir to cure his great-grandfather's illness. Why had she purposefully chosen this day?

"A lot has happened." Samuel kneeled beside Elijah and started to tell him how he had suffered.

But Elijah's large hands clasped his face tenderly and silenced him. The quilt fell from his shoulders, and Samuel was startled to see that he no longer wore the nightshirt he had put on every day. He had changed into his tasseled buckskin shirt and his prized beaded leggings, the ones decorated with porcupine quills and human hair. Both hung loosely on his debilitated body.

"Where is everyone?" Samuel asked.

"Soldiers came and told them to go to the safety of the fort, but they didn't leave right away. They stayed and looked for you," Elijah said hoarsely, then he pulled his hands back and coughed into a cotton rag. "Your father and brothers tried to find you. Your mother didn't understand why they couldn't locate you because you had only left an hour before with your friend Macduff."

"I'm sorry," Samuel said, knowing even a momentary delay could mean the difference between his family's reaching the safety of the fort walls, and death at the hands of their captors. "I knew the Shawnee were angry about the settlers breaking the treaty, but I didn't think it would come to war again. Did they get away in time?"

"I told your parents to go on," Elijah explained solemnly. His breath rattled in his chest. "But your mother's stubborn. It took a while to make her see reason."

"Why didn't you go with them?" Samuel asked.

"I stayed because I knew you would be coming home from your journey." His great-grandfather rested his hand on Samuel's shoulder, a weary look on his face.

"They didn't get away in time, did they?" Samuel said, his throat tightening against the tears. "Would they . . . could they have . . . did they stay too long on account of me?"

Elijah shook his head. The feathers in his scalp lock rustled dryly. "Don't blame yourself. Even if they had left when they were told, they wouldn't have been able to reach the fort this time."

Samuel bowed his head as guilt rushed through him. A sob worked its way up his throat and he clenched his jaw to keep from crying out. "I should have been here to help them. Maybe if I had been, we could have all made it."

"You can't think about them now," Elijah said sternly. "I have much to tell you, and you must listen carefully."

A strange numbness settled over Samuel. Tears continued to gather behind his eyes but he stoically forced them back.

"You have become worthy now."

"I failed—"

"You wouldn't listen to my way before, but now you will," Elijah went on. "For me, only hours have gone by, but for you, over two hundred years have passed."

"You know?" Samuel asked. "How do you know?"

"I have known it would happen this way since Moneto—God—gave me a vision of another world where you would be imprisoned."

"Then why didn't you stop me?" Samuel asked.

"Because I also saw the day you would go

back to that land with three other heroes to free the people who are enslaved there."

"The Legend of the Four," Samuel whispered. His quickly changing emotions made him dizzy. "I am the fourth one, but why me?"

"It is your blessing and your burden," Elijah said. "I've prayed to Moneto to bring the right words to my lips to make you understand what I am going to tell you."

Samuel inched closer until he could feel his great-grandfather's breath against his face.

"Your *unsoma* took place before you were even born," Elijah began.

An *unsoma* was the event that occurred during the first week of an infant's life and indicated the name that Moneto wanted the parents to give their child.

"I've never heard of a Shawnee named Samuel."

"Samuel is the name your mother gave you," Elijah answered.

"And how could something happen to name me before I was even born?"

"Your spirit was called from the Good in

the universe, and for that, Moneto named you Son of the Dark Goddess, the one who brings hope to the despairing."

Samuel forgot to breathe. He stared at his great-grandfather with apprehension, dreading what he would say next.

"The suffering you have been given has had a purpose," Elijah went on.

"I can't imagine any good reason for what I've been through." Samuel protested as memories of the digs came back to him.

"Every act has good and evil consequences." His great-grandfather nodded knowingly. "What you suffered will bring forth good. Without your pain Moneto wouldn't have been able to mold you into the person he needed you to become. You've shown great courage."

"What kind of courage does it take to be a slave?" Samuel asked.

"Great strength and reasoning are needed to survive enslavement," Elijah told him. "Those are traits you'll need to fulfill your purpose."

Samuel felt doubtful.

"Coyote and raven will protect and serve

you," his great-grandfather said. "They are your spirit helpers. Minor powers compared to your guardian spirit." Elijah pulled a leather strip from a fold in the quilt on his lap. Delicate stone carvings of a coyote and a raven hung on the cord, separated by wooden beads. "These are your totems. You will use them to summon your power animals." His thumb covered the last animal, as if he were waiting to reveal it.

Samuel studied the intricately engraved stones. He had seen his great-grandfather hold the objects a thousand different times, but this was the first time Samuel had been allowed to touch them.

Then Elijah removed his thumb and revealed the tiny, detailed figure of a mountain lion. "The lord of the forest is your guardian spirit, but you can't summon him," he cautioned. "Until you have the power, he will summon you."

Samuel clasped the totems and felt them squirm against his palm, as if awakened by his touch. He still had doubts, but with everything that had happened to him, he wondered how he could remain skeptical about anything magical.

"But if I see a coyote," Samuel asked after a pause. "How will I know it's my power animal and not just any creature?"

"It will speak to you," his great-grandfather answered, and a smile stretched across his tired face.

But the joy in Elijah's features didn't make Samuel happy. Instead a deep sadness shrouded him. He knew this would be the last time he would see his great-grandfather.

"You must be cautious," Elijah warned, his frail voice barely audible now. "When you were eleven I had wanted to teach you how to control the power animals, but you didn't believe in my way. Now you must learn by yourself. It can be dangerous."

Samuel pretended to scratch his eyes so Elijah couldn't see the tears trembling on his lids.

"I love you," he said and clasped his great-grandfather's bony hand.

"I can feel your love now, and you'll feel

mine forever," Elijah whispered, closing his eyes and leaning back. "But I can also sense your doubt. You think my talk is only the ramblings of a feeble old man, but everything I am telling you is true."

"It's just hard to believe I've been singled out to do something so impossible. What's so special about me?"

"I must tell you the Legend that was told to me."

"Tell me," Samuel said, anxious to hear.

Elijah paused, collecting his thoughts, and then the words came. "Four from different times will come together to mend what evil has done. Each will bring a different power to the union. But their allegiance to each other must be sworn before the day when the sun casts no shadows and the evening star's influence is strong. Then, as brothers, they will make a journey into evil's land and find the black diamond with which they will fulfill their destiny and—"

Abruptly, he stopped and cocked his head.

Samuel listened. The forest surrounding

the cabin had become unnaturally still; the Shawnee warriors were near.

"You must leave now," Elijah said.

"Come with me." Samuel started to help his great-grandfather stand. "I'll take you back to my world."

"I belong here," Elijah answered belligerently and refused to move.

"I won't go without you," Samuel said firmly.

"The choice is no longer yours. You belong in another time. You must find a way to go back and fulfill the Legend."

"Not without you," Samuel said, but he no longer felt as resolute. He could sense the truth in what Elijah had said. "Please come with me."

"Part of me already walks in the spirit land, Samuel." Elijah leaned back. "I have nothing to fear from death."

Samuel stared back at his great-grandfather and suddenly understood why Elijah had changed his dress; he wanted to die as a Shawnee, not as a frontiersman. Time slowed, and memories came to Samuel of earlier times when Elijah had taught him how to walk in the forest without making a sound and blend into the foliage without being seen. Now he wished he had spent more time listening and taking in every word. He could have learned so much more from him.

"Don't let the regrets consume you," his great-grandfather said, and closed his pale eyes, ending their last conversation.

Samuel pressed his cheek against his great-grandfather's chest, listening to his heart beat. He couldn't afford to delay the extra seconds, and yet he wasn't willing to relinquish his hold.

Outside, a whippoorwill called, but Samuel knew a man had made that sound. He jumped up and ran back outside. The sun's heat radiated off the clearing surrounding the cabin, its light blinding him. He blinked, and his vision returned. Ashley stood near the trees where he had left her, apparently unaware of the danger, and now wearing a coonskin cap.

"What?" Ashley asked, obviously concerned by the tight expression on Samuel's face.

"Nothing," Samuel answered stiffly. He kept his eyes focused on Ashley, but his mind studied the movement in his peripheral vision. He caught a glimpse of beaded moccasin. A group of Kispokotha, members of the Shawnee warrior clan, stood behind the trees, calling to each other with birdsongs.

Survival meant quick action now. He ran across the clearing, his feet hammering the hard earth.

Ashley stared at him, her eyes widening. She backed away from him. "What are you doing?"

He dove at her and they hit the ground, sliding across a mantle of leaves, twigs, and damp earth.

"It's Versace!" she shouted angrily, arms flailing.

"No, it's the Shawnee!" he shouted back, his body resting on top of hers. He tried to keep her hidden behind the thicket of blackberries, but she struggled out from under him, ripping her dress as she stood.

She slapped her hands against the back of

her short skirt. "What is it about you that likes to ruin my clothes?"

A tomahawk whizzed past her head and hit a nearby tree.

She screamed, but her shriek was drowned by half a dozen Shawnee racing from their hiding places toward them, yelling triumphantly.

"Do something!" Samuel said, and clutched the totems his grandfather had given him. If Ashley didn't open the tunnel and take them back to the future, he'd have to call up one of his power animals to save them.

He started to rub the stone coyote the way he had seen his grandfather do, but Ashley grabbed his arm, surprising him, and the totem necklace fell into a cluster of leaves.

CHAPTER FOURTEEN

A BLACK SPOT emerged from the forest shadows and pulsed toward Ashley, growing. Its force stripped tree limbs of their autumn foliage.

The Shawnee paused, their whoops diminishing into murmurs of awe.

"Come on!" Ashley yelled impatiently, yanking Samuel's shirt and trying to make him stand. "I'm not waiting a moment longer."

Frantically Samuel fanned his hands through the moldering leaves, searching for the stones. At last he found them and grabbed Ashley's elbow as she sprang into the tunnel.

Samuel looked back and caught a last glimpse of the cabin before a glaring flash sealed the opening. Then they floated, spiraling up, the speed slow and drowsy this time.

Ashley looked at him with large, mournful eyes. "I'm sorry I had to take you back to that day."

"Then why did you?" he asked, already knowing the answer, but wanting to hear it from her. What part did she play in his future?

"You needed to hear the truth from your great-grandfather," she said, "and receive your power."

"But how did you know which day to take me to?" he asked.

She looked up at him with such pity that he wondered what other secrets she was keeping from him.

"Anyone can read about you in the books on prophecy and history in Nefandus," she said quietly.

"You read about me?" he asked.

"Prophets have been predicting the end of Nefandus for ages," she went on. "The ones in power need to know everything about the Four so they can stop you before you fulfill the Legend."

"Then why was it so easy for me to escape from the digs?"

"Not everyone wants to stop the Four. Some want to use you to their own advantage. They want the powers in control now to be destroyed so they can set up their own regimes."

"The master at the dig is one of the traitors?" he asked incredulously.

"I don't know about him," she answered. "I've never met him."

Samuel paused, considering. "So which side are you on, Ashley? If you hadn't taken me back home today, then I never would have gotten my power, and the Legend wouldn't have had a chance of coming true."

He had expected a worried look to cross her face, but she didn't seem concerned that she might have betrayed the authorities in Nefandus.

"I only hurried things along," she said confidently, wrapping her hands around his waist.

"Your powers were already working, and you just weren't aware of them yet, but I couldn't wait. I need your help now, before things get too complicated in my life."

Her tone seemed so plaintive and sad that he almost felt sorry for her.

"So you think I can help you?" he asked, grabbing her other hand, pulling her against his chest as they spun steadily upward.

"I know you can."

He knew he should hate her. She had taken him back to what would have been the worst day of his life if he had lived it, but he understood the inevitability of what had just happened. His great-grandfather had been waiting for him, and if Ashley hadn't taken him back, someone else would have.

"I understand why it was essential for me to go back," he said at last, and felt the tempo of their ascent becoming slower still. "But why was it important for you to hurry things along?"

"We need to work together," she said and looked up, her eyes searching. "I know you like me."

"Not as much as you like me," he answered, brushing a hand through her hair.

She started to protest, but then she just smiled. "I do like you."

"Then tell me the secret," he said as they continued their slow spiral. "Why do you want me to work with you?"

"It's no secret," she answered bluntly. "I want to go back to my own time. Help me and we'll go back together. I can make you a king. You saw today how your life would have ended on the frontier."

"A king?" He studied her, wondering who she had been in her life before. What did Kyle know?

"Join me?" She traced one finger over his lips, and then held her face up, waiting, her body close, pressing toward him, eyes filled with desire.

He kissed her, feeling her sweet, delicate tongue touch his as her hands eased under his shirt and pulled him closer.

"Well?" she asked at last. "Will you join me?"

"Never," he whispered.

The tunnel opened without warning, and she released him. He fell onto a pile of mushy garbage. The sour, reeking smells filled his nostrils as he lost his balance and knocked his head on a rusted Dumpster.

Ashley stepped from the ring of blackness, her hair waving behind her. Her feet tapped the brick alleyway, and immediately the corridor behind her vanished with a burst of white light.

Samuel glanced around. They were back in Chinatown, in an alley behind a restaurant.

"You live too dangerously," he said and stood slowly, wanting nothing more now than to go back to the loft, think over everything that had happened, and then shower and take a long nap.

"You said you'd do anything for a trip back home."

"I don't think you lived up to your end of the bargain," he answered and hung the leather cord with the totems around his neck. "I didn't get to stay."

"I wasted all that energy and you're not going to repay me?"

He stepped closer to her and met her stare, but didn't answer her.

Frustrated, she added, "I think I'm beginning to hate you."

"No, you're not," he countered. "You're falling in love with me. I can tell by the way you were kissing me. You wanted to stay in that tunnel until we had finished a lot more than kissing."

"If you think every girl in L.A. who kisses you is in love with you, then you're in for a lot of heartache." Her annoyance with him was growing.

"I know when you're lying." He smirked and gazed down at her. "You're not as good at it as you think. And I don't know why you're so bashful about your feelings."

"I'm only using you!" She shouted angrily and then stopped, obviously realizing he had tricked her into confessing her real motive.

He smiled slyly. "How do you intend to use me, Ashley?"

She let out a breath but didn't answer.

Suddenly the back of the restaurant began

to blur, and he understood what she was doing.

"You're taking me in for a bounty?" he asked incredulously.

She didn't bother to answer.

He had meant to upset her, but not to this point. He tried to run, but there was nowhere to go; he was caught between two worlds.

CHAPTER FIFTEEN

SAMUEL RUBBED THE stone carving of the coyote totem. He had to call forth a power animal before the sticky film completely sheathed him. Once inside Nefandus, he might be able to defeat Ashley, but if she had a posse of Regulators waiting for him, escape would be impossible.

A loud crash sounded behind him. He turned to see a lumpy shadow congealing into a coyote. It tried to stand, but its forepaws slipped in the rotting food. It lay, whining, legs splayed.

Ashley paused, then burst into laughter.

"That's what your power calls forth?"

"Help me." Samuel pleaded with the mewling coyote as panic churned his stomach.

Ashley squinted, concentrating again. In moments all three of them would be in the limbo boundary between worlds, all hope gone.

The coyote sniffed, raised its head, and looked at Samuel with apologetic eyes as the gluey web crusted over its matted fur.

"Hurry," Samuel coaxed, feeling the numbness take hold. "Do something. Anything!"

The coyote quivered with a purple radiance and snarled deep in its throat. Its ears flattened back and it attacked, leaping through the glutinous air.

Ashley held her arms protectively over her face and let out a startled cry that became muffled in the dense atmosphere. She lost her concentration and the alley snapped back into focus.

"Get that mangy creature away from me!" she screamed. "It's got fleas and worms and—"

The coyote regained its balance, then crouched low, poised to jump.

Samuel laughed. "For someone who is as powerful as you pretend to be, you sure are scared of a little coyote."

"You did this," she accused.

"You expected me not to do anything?" he asked, and stepped proudly beside the tattered beast. "You were turning me in for a reward."

Ashley glanced at the scratches on her arms, then tossed Samuel a bitter and unforgiving look.

"You'll pay for this," she promised, fading into a dark silhouette. Her velvet shadow writhed up the side of the building.

Samuel studied the scruffy beast beside him and picked a burr from its coat. His great-grandfather had called forth sleek carnivores, with narrow muzzles and muscular flanks. "You sure are one sorry critter. I can't believe you're what I get for a power animal."

The coyote stared up at Samuel. *And you're what I get for a master?*

"Did you just talk to me?" Samuel asked in amazement.

The coyote opened its mouth and let out a mournful wail, ending its song with a series of short, sharp barks.

"You can't do that in this city," Samuel said and his aching loneliness overcame him again. "Trust me when I tell you that the two of us don't belong in this world. You'd better get on back to wherever you came from."

He waved his hands, trying to shoo the animal away, but it just sat down and used a back paw to scratch behind its ears. Fur and dust swirled about.

"Suit yourself." Samuel started running, hoping the coyote would go back to wherever the power animals stayed when they weren't being called forth, but when he reached the street, the coyote sped past him, its nails clattering on the sidewalk.

Shoppers stood back. A few pointed, but no one seemed to panic.

Near the entrance to the loft, Samuel paused beneath a bougainvillea to catch his breath. The over-watered earth gave off a pungent smell.

The coyote circled back and waited beside him, wagging its tail excitedly.

"We're going to have to do something about you," Samuel said, trying hard to suppress his growing affection for the animal. "My roommates aren't going to take kindly to something as flea-bitten as you are. Can you spruce yourself up a bit? Do a spell or something?"

The coyote regarded him and panted noisily in reply.

Samuel sighed, imagining the scornful look on Kyle's face when he showed up with the coyote. The animal followed him inside and sniffed at the plants as Samuel pressed the button to call the elevator. The heavy metal door slid open and Samuel entered the cage. The coyote edged back, uneasy.

"I'm going up," Samuel explained. "You can either stay or go back to your own home."

The coyote circled twice, then leaped onboard. The doors closed, barely missing its rump. It yelped as if it had been hit and skidded into the side panel.

"The door didn't even touch you," Samuel scolded. "I thought you were supposed to be brave. You're going to have to do a lot better than that if you're going to protect me."

The coyote lowered its tail in shame, and a throaty growl echoed about the small enclosure as if it were cursing.

The elevator stopped with a bump and Samuel stepped onto the landing. He pushed through the huge door to the apartment. The hearty smells of roasted squirrel and dumplings greeted him. Apparently not much time had passed since he had left to go for a run.

He hurried through the open room, hot from the sunlight, and stepped around the glass-brick wall into the kitchen.

Kyle looked up and did a double take. "You can't bring a coyote home as a pet. They come down from the hills and kill kids."

"That's not the problem," Berto said and gave Samuel a fierce look. "He just left through the back door. He didn't have enough time to go up in the hills and find a coyote."

Obie stood, his eyes looking past Samuel's

head, trying to find the magic incantation he had sent to trail Samuel. "What happened?"

"Ashley—" Samuel began.

When he had finished telling them everything about his journey back in time, they stared intently at him, each deep in his own thoughts.

Berto was the first to speak. "How do we know he's telling the truth?"

"If you don't trust what I'm saying," Samuel said. "I'll leave. Just remember, I didn't come knocking on your door seeking shelter. You kidnapped me and made me come here."

"He's telling the truth," Kyle said simply, trusting Samuel for once.

"Maybe," Berto answered, stubbornly.

Obie sighed heavily. "It was different before."

"Before?" Berto challenged, his question charged with meaning that was lost on Samuel.

"You know what I'm talking about," Obie answered.

"Before Ashley came back into our lives," Kyle blurted. "Obie is right. You don't see reason when she's involved, and every disagreement we've had lately has been because of her."

"Why do you always come back to her when things get tough?" Berto asked, but didn't wait for an answer. "She's not the one we should be focusing on now. It's Samuel. He went with her when we told him not to trust her."

"Are you guys going to let a girl come between you?" Samuel broke in, suddenly understanding the problem.

"You haven't lived with us long enough to know what we're talking about," Berto said, dismissing him.

The coyote growled deep in its throat as if it had picked up a threat in Berto's voice and was cautioning him away.

"Anyone can see," Samuel answered, petting the coyote to calm it. "It's obvious Ashley is trying to drive a wedge between the three of you . . . the four of us . . . maybe she has a reason for not wanting us to come together before the autumnal equinox."

"You were a fool to fall for her," Berto said

contemptuously, and he clenched his jaw. "She doesn't have any more feelings for you than she would have for a stray she found wandering on the street."

"I'm not in love with her," Samuel shouted back. "You are, and you're putting all your emotions on me so you'll have a convenient place to hate them."

"I'm not the one who just kissed her." Berto stepped closer, his fingers curling into a fist.

The coyote bared its teeth and its ears went flat against its skull.

"I kissed her, but that's nothing special with a girl like her. She kisses any guy who will let her," Samuel said and immediately regretted his words.

CHAPTER SIXTEEN

SAMUEL HURRIED down the outside corridor at Turney High, swinging a crumpled brown bag. Voices and laughter echoed around him as other students joined their friends for lunch. The savory smells from the cafeteria made his stomach rumble.

A week had passed and the purple bruise from Berto's punch had faded to a greenish yellow, but the tension in the loft hadn't diminished. Samuel didn't know how to mend the rift with Berto. Every time he tried he seemed only to make Berto angrier.

Samuel needed a wilderness where he could run free and clear his mind to think, but on his last visit, Griffith Park had been crowded with families picnicking, sunbathing, and throwing Frisbees—hardly a place for solitude.

He stopped abruptly. He hadn't watched where he was going and now he was inches from Ashley. He saw her every day at school, so she knew where to find him. Still, no Regulators had been sent to capture him, and that bothered him. What was she waiting for? When the Shawnee became too quiet, homesteaders always knew an attack was eminent.

He had shared his concerns with Obie and Kyle, but they didn't sense the pressure building the way he did.

Now Ashley glanced up and saw him. A spark of contempt fired her gaze. She leaned against Sledge and kissed his cheek, leaving a pink imprint of her lips on him, then tucked her hands under his shirt and slid her palms possessively over his abdomen. Samuel didn't understand why she was trying to make him jealous, but then he saw her real target. Berto leaned against a locker, glaring at Sledge and Ashley. Finally Kyle joined him and the two walked toward the back of the school.

Changing direction, Samuel pushed through the throng of kids and went the long way around to the quad. He started searching for an empty bench where he could sit and eat his lunch.

Maddie was sitting at a table by herself, reading and scribbling notes on a yellow pad with a purple pen. Jeweled barrettes held her hair away from her face, and the curls fell on her back, fluttering in the breeze. His heart pounded with indecision. If he walked over to her, would she even speak to him?

"How's your friend Emily doing?" he said, straddling the bench and setting his bag on the table.

She looked up with a start and flushed. "Emily is doing very well, thank you. She'll be coming back to school in another month maybe."

"So you vanquished the vampire?" he asked, trying to be jovial. He pulled a peanut butter-and-chocolate chip sandwich from his bag.

Maddie folded her arms over her book, her silence dismissing him.

"I'm sorry Ashley upset you," he said, working his mouth around the words he had practiced all week. "Do you think we could start over? I'd like to be your friend."

"Right," she said with annoyance. "You want to be with me now that Sledge has taken Ashley from you."

"That's not it," he countered.

"I'm not second best. Go find a girl who doesn't mind dating Ashley's rejects." Her tone was nasty, but the hurt in her eyes exposed her real feelings. She slammed her book shut and dropped it into her backpack.

"It was so great chatting with you," she said sarcastically and stood. "Now I have to go."

"Where?" he said quickly. "I'll go with you."

"I need to be alone," she answered. She walked away without turning back to look at him.

"Fine," he grumbled, leaving and left his

lunch for the seagulls. He started toward the soccer field. Cutting classes was the only thing he had mastered during his first week at school, and that was exactly what he intended to do right now.

Obie had been schooled in Nefandus, and studying was easy for him, but Samuel had spent his time in the caves, digging, sweating, and blistering his hands. He hadn't been prepared for this world. What education he did have he had received from his mother, who had been a teacher before marrying his father.

He picked up his pace, turned the corner, and nearly bumped into Berto and Kyle. They leaned against the back fence, eating tacos and watching guys playing soccer, but Samuel knew they had been waiting for him.

Berto grinned. "Do you like this game?" he asked, motioning toward the soccer field.

It was the first time Berto had spoken to Samuel since their fight.

Samuel shrugged. "I like running better."

"We had a game like this back in my time," Berto continued. "The object was to get the ball into the end zones, same as they're playing it now, but we could only hit the ball with our hips, knees, and elbows. But the best difference was that in our game, the winner got to kill his opponent. Maybe you and I should play some-day."

"Maybe we could settle a few things." Samuel took up the challenge.

Kyle cleared his throat as if reminding Berto of something.

Berto nodded and went on in hushed tones, "Kyle says I have to talk to you about Ashley before the autumnal equinox." Ordinarily Berto was strong and confident, but now he seemed unsure. Samuel waited. "Ashley and I met in the digs," Berto said softly. "We made our plans and escaped together, but she couldn't adjust to life in L.A."

That surprised Samuel. If anyone seemed to relish the crazy life here, Ashley did.

Berto stared out at the playing field and continued. "She wanted to go back to her home in Mesopotamia. Finally she discovered that if she became a bounty hunter, the members of the Inner Circle would reward her with the power of time travel not all at once, just a little at a time, some for each *servus* she returned."

Samuel sensed that Berto had been tempted to join her and that part of him still was.

"She awakened bad things inside me," Berto said. He seemed uncomfortable with his confession. "She triggered impulses I try to keep hidden." Berto frowned, and Samuel sensed the darkness inside him. "I had to let her go."

"You did the right thing," Kyle put in, his eyes never leaving the soccer match.

"But letting her go didn't stop the feelings I had for her," he continued. "I hadn't seen her for a long time, and then suddenly she was back, going to high school here, using the same front as mine." He cursed under his breath and started to speak again.

"You don't need to say more," Samuel interrupted. It was obvious Berto still loved Ashley in spite of what she had become.

"Let's ditch this place," Berto said, but

he didn't wait for them. He turned abruptly and started walking toward the parking lot.

"I'm with you," Samuel said and headed after him, but Kyle grabbed his arm, stopping him.

"Let Berto go. He needs to be alone and you need to stay," Kyle said. "I have something to show you after school."

"Can't you show me now?" Samuel asked and looked back at the long line of dreary buildings. He didn't want to spend another sunny afternoon boxed inside a stuffy classroom with no windows.

"Sorry," Kyle said with a slim smile. "It has to be after class."

At the end of the day, Samuel followed Kyle down the outside of the auditorium. Heat radiated off the stucco wall, and behind them basketballs hit the asphalt with a steady smack.

"This won't be the same as running through the wilderness," Kyle explained. "But I thought you might like to go out for track."

"Track?" Samuel asked.

"Come on," Kyle said excitedly and headed

past the metal bleachers. Twenty guys were running endlessly around a dirt path that encircled the football field.

Kyle hurried over to a large, red-faced man whose belly hung over his belt. Thin black hair barely covered his sunburned scalp.

Kyle stopped in front of the man. "Coach Haddock, this is Samuel, the guy I was telling you about."

Coach Haddock inspected him, his fat fingers playing over a silver whistle hanging around his neck, but it was the sensation of other eyes watching him that made Samuel look back at the bleachers.

Maddie sat alone, gazing at the field, her feet resting on the seat in front of her, showing off her beautiful, tanned legs.

"So, what do you say?"

Samuel turned back, suddenly aware that Coach Haddock had been talking to him.

"You don't need to race full bore. Just go out there and burn up the track," Coach Haddock went on.

Samuel stared at him, wondering what he was

saying. He looked to Kyle for an explanation.

Kyle shoved him. "Go run the track."

"You want me to run in circles?" Samuel asked, trying to understand.

Guys in baggy shorts sprinted around the circular race course. They looked winded and bored.

"Race the other guys," Kyle said. "See Sledge over there? Go kick his butt for Berto."

"You want me to kick—"

"It's an expression," Kyle corrected. "Race him and win."

Running in circles didn't make a lot of sense to Samuel, but he slipped out of his shoes anyway and started off slowly. His feet slapped out a steadily increasing rhythm. He glanced at Maddie and found a faster pace. Soon he overtook the others and sprinted past Sledge. His mind drifted, and he was back on the frontier, reliving his earlier life with Macduff.

Coach Haddock blew his whistle. "Shower up," he shouted.

It took Samuel a moment to realize the others had stopped running and were walking across the grassy center of the track. He chased after them, sorry the session had ended, and glanced up at the bleachers, but Maddie had left.

Coach Haddock rested his hand on Sledge's shoulder and looked at Samuel. "It's been a long time since you've had any competition."

Sledge wheezed and gave Samuel a cold stare. "I'm just suffering from the running flats."

"Then Samuel will get you pumped back up." The coach smiled as if he had just won a sought-after prize.

"I'll show you tomorrow," Sledge promised. But his voice sounded uncertain. He ran off to the locker room.

Coach Haddock stayed behind while Samuel slipped back into his shoes.

"Good work," Coach Haddock congratulated him. "But you have to buy the right kind of shoes. Those won't work, and I can't let you run barefoot." Then he handed Samuel three sheets of paper. "Fill these out, have your parents sign them, and bring them back tomorrow."

Samuel pretended to study the papers for a long time, hoping Maddie would return. Finally he stuffed the papers into his back pocket and walked to the locker room. He eased along the bank of lockers, wondering where the others had gone. The steamy air smelled of sweat, wet towels, and deodorant sprays. He didn't think they could have changed and left so quickly, but the vaulted room felt completely empty and too quiet.

A distant snap echoed and the overhead lights went out. Murky darkness surrounded him. He stared at the wraithlike shadow near the entrance, unsure. If Regulators hovered there, they had learned to control the electrical energy that had always heralded their appearance before. But something was definitely trying to form.

He pinched his totem expectantly.

The dark cloud squirmed, wiggled, and flickered, at last becoming dense.

CHAPTER SEVENTEEN

"**M**ACDUFF!" SAMUEL hollered and ran to him. He wrapped his arms around his friend and lifted him off the ground.

Macduff cried out.

"What's wrong?" Samuel set him down.

"The Regulators returned me to the master." Macduff lifted his shirt and showed Samuel the bleeding whip marks that crisscrossed his back.

"It was dangerous for you to come find me," Samuel said, admiring his friend's bravery.

"I had to come," Macduff whispered. "After the master beat me, he left me unconscious. But when I came to, I heard him talking about you with one of the ministers from the city."

"Me?" Samuel felt his stomach drop. "What did they say?"

Macduff started to answer, but Samuel held up his hand. The peculiar sense of being watched had come over him again. He listened, vigilant; his muscles tensed; he was ready to flee.

Water dripped in the shower stalls. The ceiling beams creaked. No sound suggested that others were in the building, but Samuel couldn't shake the feeling that someone was hiding in the dark, spying on him.

"Let's go," he whispered, and took Macduff's arm.

Minutes later they sat at a small round table in glaring sunshine, drinking coffee, surrounded by Hollywood wannabes talking about casting calls and new head shots. Samuel sipped the bitter brew. He liked the aroma better than the taste. Macduff stirred sugar into his cup, and the twirling spoon clicked the sides, but when he finished, he didn't drink. He had a jittery nervousness about him, and his hands trembled too severely to lift the cup. He clasped the edge of the table as if he were trying to stop the twitching.

"Are you okay?" Samuel asked. "Maybe we should find a doctor."

"I'm fine," Macduff answered, but Samuel could see the panic in his eyes. "Do you know what we were looking for in the digs?" Macduff asked finally.

"You know I don't," Samuel answered impatiently. None of the *servi* had ever known, and anyone who had had the nerve to ask had been punished. Samuel had never seen coal or any precious metal pulled from the dirt, but daily he and others had shoveled deeper and carried more red clay to the surface.

"All that fuss was over a black diamond," Macduff said.

"The black diamond," Samuel repeated, remembering his great-grandfather's words. "Are you sure?"

Macduff nodded.

"Tell me everything." Samuel set his coffee aside and leaned closer.

"The black diamond once belonged to the ruler of Nefandus," Macduff said, his eyes flitting nervously from side to side. "But during a battle before the creation of time, the diamond broke loose from its crown. They've been trying to recover it since. They've dug until the mines have made a honeycomb out of the mountains. They need its power to invade the earth realm."

"Why didn't they just cast a spell to find it?" Samuel wondered aloud. "The whole place runs on magic. You'd think they could have found an easier way."

"It can't be summoned," Macduff answered excitedly. He reached for his cup, but when he lifted it, coffee sloshed over the top. He set it down and hid his hands beneath the table. "It has too much power."

"You said they were talking about me," Samuel probed. "What did they say?"

"I kept going in and out of consciousness,"

Macduff explained, breathing deeply as if the memory upset him. "They mentioned your name, and next they were talking about the diamond."

"Try to remember more."

"Why?" Macduff shrugged, and then he flinched as if the movement had caused him pain. "We got the information we need. I know where to find the black diamond."

Samuel's heart took on a faster rhythm, and his blood throbbed in his temples. "Where?"

"The master has it."

"Are you sure he still has it?" Samuel asked. "He should have turned it over by now."

"The old fool isn't going to give it to authorities," Macduff answered. "He and the minister are planning to keep it for themselves. I know where they hid it, and if we can steal it, we'll be able to return to our own time."

Samuel pulled back, remembering what his great-grandfather had told him about his destiny. He wanted to go home. That was all he had thought about since his first day in captivity, but now he knew he couldn't. He stared at the people walking down the street, living ordinary lives, and his heart filled with bitter envy. Maybe he should forget everything and go back with Macduff. They could steal the diamond and finally get home. But then he thought of the *servi* living in the dusty pits, breathing the sulfur vapors, their hands cut and gnarled. He couldn't turn his back on them, no matter how much he had to sacrifice.

"You don't want to stay in this world, do you?" Macduff asked. "Wouldn't you rather go back to our own time and live on the frontier?"

"Sure," Samuel answered. "But I don't have that luxury now, and even if we go back. it won't be what we remember. We're changed now. You said it yourself."

"Haven't you heard a thing I've been telling you?" Macduff said irritably. Then, with obvious effort, he controlled his frustration and spoke calmly. "The diamond gives us the power to do anything we want. We could even go back and forth between eras. We could—"

"I have to check with my friends first," Samuel interrupted.

"We don't need anyone to help us," Macduff argued.

"Come with me." Samuel stood. "You can tell them what you've told me."

Macduff pulled out a watch like the one he had given Samuel. He clicked it open and studied the face, checking the astrological time. "I'll wait for you at the portal where you came through."

"I can't promise we'll meet you there."

"Then I'll return on my own." Macduff looked at Samuel as if something terrible were troubling him. "You're my truest friend."

The words made Samuel pause. "You say that like you're standing over my grave."

"I just want you to know how much your friendship means to me." Macduff went on, unsmiling. "You've never let me down."

CHAPTER EIGHTEEN

"**H**OW DO YOU know the things Macduff told you are true?" Kyle asked, wincing as the makeup artist plucked a hair from between his brows.

"I trust him," Samuel answered, squinting against the beaming lightbulbs bordering the mirrors. The piercing fumes from hairsprays, dyes, and depilatory creams caused his eyes to water. Behind him a hairdresser ran a blow-dryer over a girl's wet hair, and the heat made sweat prickle across his forehead.

"All right, then," Kyle said, but he didn't

seem happy about his decision. He tore off the white tissue tucked neatly around his collar.

"Where are you going?" The makeup artist pointed an eyebrow brush at Kyle. "I'm not done."

Kyle jumped from the chair and kissed her cheek. "Sorry, I'll mention your name when I win my first Oscar."

"You can't leave." Her eyes widened in surprise. "Kyle, this is the opportunity you've been waiting for. Everyone dreams of—"

"I know," he cut her off and left the trailer.

Samuel followed him into the cooler air outside. The sun had set, and deep purple clouds streaked across the horizon, silhouetting the tall palm trees.

"They were giving me a line tonight," Kyle brooded as they ambled between buzzing generators. "Do you know what that means?"

Samuel had no idea.

"I'd get a SAG card." He paused in front of the honey wagon. "That means membership in the Screen Actors Guild. Do you know how important that is?"

Samuel shook his head and Kyle started forward again, hurrying past the plush coaches that housed the stars.

"In this town it's everything if you want to be an actor," Kyle said as they ran across the street to a parking area. "You have to have a speaking part before you can get into the Screen Actors Guild, and you can't get a speaking part unless you're already a guild member."

Samuel puzzled over Kyle's statement. "That's ridiculous."

"Not to me." He pounded his fist on his car fender and gazed cheerlessly back at the set. Men and women were positioning an array of lights on scaffolding high overhead.

"Seems to me we're all giving up something we want," Samuel said, reminded disconsolately of his family.

Kyle sighed and opened his car door. "You said the black diamond can grant any wish."

"That's what Macduff implied." Samuel slipped into the car and slammed the door.

"Then I'm going to wish for an Oscar." Kyle slid behind the steering wheel and turned the key in the ignition. The engine rumbled. He yanked the steering wheel and slammed his foot on the gas pedal. Tires screamed, a bluish vapor filled the car with the smell of burned rubber, and they sped away, setting off car alarms in their wake.

By the time they arrived at Club Quake, Kyle had spent his anger. He seemed subdued, almost depressed, as if his thoughts had turned to the danger that lay before them. He maneuvered his car between two stretch limos; the chauffeurs watched him warily.

"I still don't understand why it has to be tonight," he said, turning his attention back to Samuel.

"Macduff didn't say, but I imagine he's afraid the master will hide the diamond in a different place. This could be our one and only chance."

"All right, then." Kyle climbed from the car and crossed the street toward a large, windowless building. A muffled *thump, thump, thump* came from the techno music inside. Kids were lined up, three and four abreast, waiting to enter the club.

Berto stood behind a burgundy velvet rope that was suspended between silver stanchions. He was dressed in black, and his hair was slicked back. A diamond sparkled in one earlobe; a small plastic headset curled over his other ear. He started to smile, but when he caught their troubled expressions, he became solemn. "What's up?"

"You have to come with us," Kyle said.

"Right," Berto interrupted before Kyle could explain and nodded back at the growing line. "And have pandemonium break loose. I'm the gatekeeper."

"Samuel's friend Macduff knows where we can find the black diamond." Kyle leaned closer. "We're going into Nefandus and stealing it tonight."

Berto tore off his headset and slung it around his neck. "How do you know where to locate it?"

Samuel repeated what Macduff had told him, but Berto remained more skeptical than Kyle.

"How do you know we can trust Macduff?"

he asked, holding up his hand to stop three guys from sneaking into the club.

"He's got the whip marks on his back to prove his story," Samuel answered. "I saw them."

Berto stared at him as if a thousand questions were flashing through his mind, but then at last he said resolutely, "We need to find Obie, but he's probably on stage already, and there's no way you'll be able to talk him into leaving."

"I'll decide that." Obie stood near the huge front door, his long blond hair falling over his massive shoulders. "The runes warned me that tonight would be dangerous. What's up?"

Samuel tried to tell Obie what he had already told Berto and Kyle, but the kids in line were becoming impatient. They yelled, trying to get Berto's attention, and the noise drowned out Samuel's voice.

"I don't need to hear more," Obie said and looked up at the constellation of Perseus as if checking the time. "We need to hurry. Just let me tell the band they'll be performing without me."

Minutes later, they drove toward Santa Monica in worried silence. When they reached the beach, the four friends got out of the car and walked down the shoreline near Ashley's house. Wind rustled their hair and slapped their clothes. They paused at the water's edge.

"Macduff said he'd wait for us," Samuel said, his apprehension building. "I don't understand why he isn't here."

"Maybe Ashley caught him," Berto said glumly.

"We should have gone to a different portal," Kyle said, his voice strained. "One we know better."

Obie stared up at the night sky. "It's starting."

The wind stopped. The atmosphere became dense and sluggish, as if the air had thickened to a paste. Breathing grew more difficult. A glow spread across the sand, becoming brighter, and the soft light glinted off the waves in a rainbow spray.

"Don't stay bunched together," Obie whispered. "Spread out in case it's a trap so they'll have a harder time catching us."

Samuel caught movement in the corner of his eye. His heart skipped a beat. Ashley stood with Macduff, wearing a long velvet cape, the shoulders decorated with insignia and crests.

He hadn't heard them approaching, and that worried him. Macduff was hunched over, as if the pain from the wounds on his back had become excruciating. Samuel started forward to help him, but a sudden crack of thunder made him stop. Electrical sparks danced across the shore.

"You turned us in!" Samuel's anger overcame his fear. He lunged at Macduff, ready to pummel him, but before he could strike, Ashley spun her finger, and a thousand thin threads swaddled him.

Obie wrote runic symbols in the air and sent an incantation buzzing toward Ashley. She waved her hand and his letters broke apart, sprinkling over the sand.

"Please," she said with regal command, her cape fluttering as she stepped forward. "You can't defeat me—"

"Yet," Berto put in, the determination in his expression matching her own.

"Don't delude yourself, Berto." Ashley stared at him, her eyes fiery, and in the dim light Samuel couldn't tell if her gaze was one of intense love or hate. "It'll never happen now. Your time has run out. Macduff helped me capture you. I didn't think you'd fall for something so obvious. The whipping was his idea. A masterful touch."

"I never figured you for a turncoat." Samuel glared at Macduff.

"I'm no traitor. I'm looking out for you and me. What do we care what happens to these others?" Macduff asked. "They're no friends of ours, and you said yourself you'd do anything to go home."

"Not this way," Samuel answered.

"I'm being more loyal than you are," Macduff said fiercely, not backing down. "Ashley took me home. I saw what happened to our families, and Ashley's the only one who can help us now. She'll take us back one day earlier. Think of it. One day is enough time to convince our families to leave for the fort."

"You saw how easy it is for me to take you back," Ashley said convincingly. "I'll do it in exchange for the black diamond."

Samuel felt his chest tighten. "And if I don't?"

"You'll share the fate of Obie, Berto, and Kyle." She frowned. "I'll turn you over to Regulators."

"You have the chance right here to save your family," Macduff said furiously. "If you don't go with me, you'll be murdering your own kin."

CHAPTER NINETEEN

"**W**HAT DO YOU say?" Macduff asked and tried to smile.

"I can't," Samuel answered. Guilt gnawed at him. He swallowed hard and blinked back burning tears. He loved his family and wanted to be with them, but he had to fulfill his destiny. "I'm staying, and you should have chosen more wisely. Ashley's deserting you already."

Macduff snapped around. Ashley was rising into the portal. A golden aura quivered around her, making her dangerous beauty even more compelling.

"Are you turning me over with the rest of them?" Macduff asked plaintively.

"Without Samuel, you're no use to me," Ashley explained and blew him a kiss.

As soon as she had disappeared, thunder boomed and the night prickled with electricity. The fine hairs on Samuel's neck stood on end.

"Regulators," Berto whispered. "Do we leave or fight?"

"We stay," Obie commanded. "The portal remains open for a while. Maybe we can sneak around them as they're coming through."

"He's right," Kyle said. "We need to go into Nefandus tonight. It could be our only chance to get the diamond."

"You're fools, all of you," Macduff said bitterly. "These Regulators won't be gatekeepers. They'll be the elite guards. I know what Ashley was planning."

The others ignored him, but Samuel scowled and whispered coldly, "You're a coward."

"Suit yourself," Macduff answered. "You're not going to be able to fight them off."

"Which way are they coming?" Kyle asked, surveying the waves.

Thunder exploded again, rattling the ground. A tremor ran down the beach and vibrated up Samuel's legs and, in the same moment, a dense cloud poured from the air and settled over them, churning like thick, dark fog. The noxious fumes seeped into Samuel's lungs. He coughed and choked.

Macduff stumbled against him, wheezing. "I'm sorry," he said in a hoarse voice. "I should have known not to trust her. I never meant to betray you. I thought I was helping."

"It's too late for apologies," Samuel said, his throat burning. "Your actions already spoke for you."

The black vapors began compressing into man-size shapes, and with a jolt Samuel realized he had been breathing the dematerialized bodies of Regulators. He gagged and tried to quell his need to retch.

Berto cursed and spit.

"There must be ten or more materializing. We'd better retreat." Obie had started to change. The lower half of his body blurred with the dark, but before he could transform, jagged blue sparks crackled over his face. Simultaneously the grotesque head of a Regulator took shape beside Obie, and then a burly body formed. The monster hunkered over Obie, grinning maniacally.

Samuel, Kyle, and Berto dashed toward Obie to help, but he shook his head. "Save yourself. Get away while you can."

Another thunderclap resounded and ripped the sky. The ground was still trembling as more shadows hissed through the portal and spread out in a meandering haze.

"Now! We've got to leave now!" Kyle screamed. "She's sent an army after us."

"I can't," Samuel yelled back. He didn't understand what was weighting him down. He only had seconds to disappear, but he couldn't muster the power. He heard panicked breathing louder than his own and felt someone pinching his arm. Macduff was holding on to him. Their eyes locked.

"I can't take you," Samuel said. Guilt and

sorrow made his stomach tighten. "I can't." He shook his arm free.

Macduff staggered back, whimpering. Immediately, three Regulators descended upon him, dissolving him into their shadows, and carried him back through the portal.

Samuel watched, ashamed; Macduff had once been his best friend, but he couldn't consider his grief for long. More Regulators arose from the ominous cloud. Two came forward and seized Berto before he could run. Samuel ran to help him but a shadow wrapped around his arm, holding him back. The clammy touch made his skin crawl and leeched his strength. He struggled against the Regulator's hold, but it was like wrestling a breeze.

From his peripheral vision, he saw Berto project his spirit from his body in a last and futile attempt to escape. An opaque vapor swept around his ghostly image, forcing his soul back into his body. Berto's eyes flashed open, and widened with terror as Regulators whisked him up and back through the gate into Nefandus.

Now the phantom holding Samuel

materialized. His foul breath puffed over Samuel's face. Samuel pinched the stone talisman hanging around his neck and frantically rubbed it.

At once a primeval howl shattered the night. The Regulator paused, as if trying to identify the wail, his rheumy eyes searching.

The coyote crouched, teeth bared, and growled, then sprung, its hind legs kicking sand as it hurtled itself at the Regulator. Its jaws clenched the Regulator's sagging neck, but before its teeth could do damage, the Regulator burst into a thousand fragments. The coyote fell on the beach with a loud thump.

The attack gave Samuel the seconds he needed. He ran down the beach, his feet crushing shells and slippery kelp. Behind him a volley of yells and growls filled the night. He couldn't turn back to see what was happening, because three dark apparitions wavered near him. The shadows snaked around his hands, arms and cheeks, and their mists bubbled painfully over his skin as the creatures tried to melt into him and make him disappear.

CHAPTER TWENTY

SAMUEL DASHED headlong into the surf, hoping the ocean spray would mix with the shadowy Regulators clinging to him and loosen their grip. He continued sprinting through the foaming waves, trying to free himself from their black, vaporous forms. Water splashed around him, and then the running did for him what it always had. His mind relaxed and he was able to transform. The night cradled him, and he shot into the sky, a plume of silky smoke, surprising his captors and slipping from their hold. He swerved away from the ocean and sped toward the abandoned church where he had spent his first night, hoping to find refuge there.

His vision was panoramic now, and each shade and shape became distinct, but his feeling of safety quickly left him. Four Regulators chased after him, gaining on him at terrifying speed. Their ebony silhouettes stretched like glossy cirrus clouds strafing in front of the crescent moon.

The winds gusted and blew Samuel off course, toward the north. He glanced down at the streets winding up the canyon below him. From his vantage point it was easy to see that the houses were built in an old creek bed. That gave him hope. Storm waters had to drain someplace. In this newfangled world the government thought it did better than nature. Somewhere nearby there had to be a drain for the runoff from the rains so that the houses wouldn't wash away. He dove and skimmed over the treetops. If he could find the culvert, then he'd find a little bit of wilderness.

In front of him, a slab of concrete gleamed as white as bleached bones. He followed it to the crest of the hill and glided into a heavily wooded area behind the housing tract.

Samuel materialized, running as he formed, his steps sure on the slippery pine needles. He crept into the thicker brush, without turning a leaf or breaking a twig, and hid. Behind him, Regulators started to take shape, their huge bodies tottering on the steep slope. Their evil presence silenced the chirping crickets and frogs. A smaller Regulator stepped into the poison ivy, then turned, startled by a raccoon, and lost his balance. He tumbled down the hill, his corona of electric sparks igniting a series of small fires in the dry pine needles.

With so much kindling, the fires joined each other rapidly and advanced in a steady line up the hill. Acrid smoke whirled and wreathed the tall pine trees. The other Regulators regarded the blaze. Their expressions suggested they were communicating telepathically.

Samuel waited, leaves smoldering around him, their fumes seeping into his nose.

The fire must have convinced them that he had somehow escaped. They trundled down to their fallen comrade, then vanished, carrying the wounded Regulator with them.

Sirens filled the night and the flames crackled nosily, but Samuel remained motionless. He feared the departure of the Regulators had only been a ploy. He remained hiding until flames licked his shoes and the blaze shot up, singeing his eyebrows and scorching the front of his shirt. At last, coughing and gasping for air, he crawled from his hiding place

A terrible fear rose inside him. In spite of the heat, he began to shiver. He dreaded going back to Nefandus alone, but he couldn't live with himself if he didn't try to rescue the others. He glanced up at the constellation of Perseus, wondering how long he'd have to wait before the portal opened again. He prayed it would open in time for him to save his friends.

CHAPTER TWENTY-ONE

THREE DAYS LATER, Samuel left the apartment and headed toward the old Chinatown gateway. He hurried past the red, pagoda-style buildings and stopped in front of IT PUN FORTUNE READING.

Samuel stared at his nervous reflection in the plate-glass storefront and swallowed hard. He couldn't use the portal at the beach—Ashley would have Regulators waiting for him there. But Kyle had told him that another gate opened here, in the fortune-teller's shop.

He flipped open the pocket watch and searched the cluster of stars beneath the crystal until he found the constellation of Perseus. The eye of Medusa had already begun to fade. He glanced up and his stomach churned. He was positive this was the place Kyle had pointed out, yet he felt no change in the atmosphere as he had at the beach. A breeze continued to ruffle his clothes, and the only glow came from a flickering pink neon light.

No one around him seemed to notice anything strange. Shoppers hurried in and out of the bakery, releasing the fresh-bread smells when they opened the door, and a group of tourists with nametags pinned to their shoulders strolled down the walk, talking noisily and peering into the souvenir shops.

Maybe he hadn't remembered correctly. There should have been some preternatural sign that the gate between the two worlds had opened. He paced, undecided. Time was running out. He turned back, resolute, then let out a war cry and charged toward the window. Somewhere behind him a woman screamed. A chorus of horrified wails and gasps followed.

Samuel hit the storefront and grimaced, expecting shards of glass to rip open his flesh.

Instead, sound became muffled. The crowd blurred, and then the store disappeared. He found himself suspended in an unpleasant casing, unable to breathe. Numbness crept through his body as his atoms reconfigured. He remained frozen until a slow, dull ache awakened his senses, and then he stumbled forward, crashing into a gray brick wall. He smelled the cloyingly sweet odor from the magic fires and knew he was back in Nefandus. He turned slowly, his muscles tense and ready for running, but the street on which he found himself was empty.

Gargoyles peered down at him. Their stony eyes followed him as he walked past the tall, narrow houses. Steeples pierced the bright sky, each turret rising higher than the one before. Samuel wasn't familiar with the city, but the homes seemed abandoned.

At a crossroads he paused, not knowing

which way to go, and then, from a bell tower, a raven cawed and flew down at him. He ducked. The bird's glossy feathers brushed mischievously against his forehead as it swept past. The soft *whoosh* of its flapping was the only sound in the stillness.

"Have you come to show me the way?" Samuel asked, his voice filled with awe and respect.

As if in answer, the bird abruptly turned back, wings spread. It glided low beneath the balconies, then continued close to the ground.

At the next street, the bird took its time, hopping from branch to gnarled branch in a row of stunted trees, and even when it flew, it stayed low.

"I can run faster than this," Samuel complained, his anxiety growing.

The raven perched. It cackled and clucked as if scolding him, then twitched and looked up.

Samuel glanced at the gauzy sky and caught his breath. Hundreds upon hundreds of shadows flowed in one direction, leaving the city and flocking to the countryside.

He might have thought some disaster had occurred from which the residents were fleeing, but he knew instinctively that they were heading toward the amphitheater. The *servi* in the digs had spoken in frightened whispers about the sacrifices that took place there twice a year. He started to fade to join the others, but the raven pecked his head.

"Ouch!" he yelled, rubbing his scalp, but he understood at once. If he transformed he could accidentally brush through the shadow of a powerful master and be identified.

Samuel started running instead, and twenty minutes later he stood in front of the huge amphitheater that was encrusted with gleaming white marble. Shadows were still streaming overhead, landing on the highest tier and forming into men and women. People milled around the top arcade, their animated chatter rising as Samuel crept forward and entered through an archway on the ground floor.

He ran down the elaborately decorated passageway, sprinting past gleaming sculptures and mosaics. A soft roar came through the massive stone wall as he started up a steep staircase. Applause followed.

At the top he stepped through an arch onto a covered walkway and stopped abruptly. Spectators crowded the area, talking, laughing, and eating as they waited for the entertainment to begin. He hid behind a large, elegant woman and bowed his head, pretending to be her *servus*, then eased to the side and peered around a column. Rows of seats circled a huge, sunbaked arena.

Members of the Inner Circle were already settled beneath billowing canopies of red, orange, and purple silk. They gossiped and read the programs that listed the names and offenses of the Renegades and *servi* to be executed. Other *servi* crouched nervously beside their masters, their eyes wide with terror, aware even in their drugged stupor that one day they might be the victims waiting to be sacrificed.

Four main entrances led into the arena, with numerous smaller passages between them. People were leaning over the railing trying to see into the dark openings, yelling and taunting the prisoners. Samuel sensed immediately that his friends were down there somewhere. He had to find a way to get into the maze of corridors in the basement and find them.

A black smudge caught his attention and he looked back at the audience. Two velvet shadows brushed over the spectators and hovered above empty seats. The darker cloud reformed into a tall, distinguished gentleman with prominent cheekbones set in a thin, cruel face. Samuel froze, surprised to see his master from the digs.

The gossamer silhouette accompanying him undulated as if it were primping. Then Ashley materialized. She scanned the audience, searching, as if she sensed Samuel's presence. She turned in his direction, but the master stood suddenly with the other spectators and blocked her view.

Samuel jerked backward, his heart thumping painfully in his chest. Ashley had lied to him about knowing the master. But before he could consider this further, trumpets sounded and everyone rushed to their seats, their voices rising in anticipation. Samuel was left alone in the walkway. He ventured a look around the column again.

Regulators marched into the stadium, sending a tremor of excitement through the crowd. Everyone seemed to adore and respect the evil-looking creatures. The yells rose to an unrelentingly high pitch as the better-known Regulators entered the ring. Their long cloaks, emblazoned with medals and awards, hung crookedly over their misshapen bodies.

Finally the procession ended. The audience settled back as the Regulators exited through the arches in the sides of the ring, and the first of the condemned Renegades was pushed into the arena.

A thin girl with knotted scars on her back looked up at the audience. Her hana berry juice had been withheld, and without its numbing affects, she was aware of what was about to happen. She began to shriek, and the small boy next to her put his arms around her and tried to comfort her. The audience laughed. Their thunderous voices shook the building.

Samuel knew the combat would never be fair, but fairness didn't seem to matter to the crowd. Their anticipation of the public executions only grew.

He hurried back the way he had come. At the bottom of the stairs, he ran down a long corridor and took the first side passageway, hoping to find a staircase that would take him down to the holding area and his friends.

Without warning, someone clutched his arm and pulled him into an alcove.

CHAPTER TWENTY-TWO

MADDIE STOOD IN a recessed archway, shivering, her fingers fidgeting with the hem of her skirt. Her chest rose and fell rapidly as she took in sharp, shallow breaths.

"Maddie?" Samuel took off his jean jacket and placed it around her shoulders. A million questions raced through his mind.

"I'm so glad to see you," she said, slipping her arms into the sleeves. She tried to work the buttons, but her hands fumbled and she finally gave up. "Everything you told me that night in the graveyard is true."

"How did you get in here?" he asked, buttoning the jacket.

"After track practice, I tried to find you." She paused. Her cheeks, already flushed from crying, turned crimson. "I wanted to tell you I was sorry for acting so rude—"

"You did?" Unexpected happiness momentarily pushed aside his fear.

She nodded. "Then I saw you talking to someone in the locker room and you called him Macduff," she said. "So, of course, I followed you both to Cafe Olé."

"Did you hear what we said?" he asked.

She nodded again and new tears formed on her lids. "That's why I trailed you to the movie set and then to Club Quake." She paused, and her chin quivered.

For a moment he thought she was going to break down, but then she continued. "At the beach, after those shadow creatures captured Kyle, Obie, and Berto, I went down to the shore to figure out what happened, but then one of the monsters caught me and brought me here." She shuddered, her teeth chattering.

He pulled her against him, and tried to warm her with his body.

"I always wondered what people meant when they said they felt as if they had walked into a nightmare." Her lips moved against his chest as she spoke. "Now I know, and it sucks."

"Maddie," he said quietly, smoothing her hair from her face. "Can you show me where Obie, Kyle, and Berto are being held?"

"Yes." Her voice was trembling, but when she looked up at him, her gaze was resolute. "They attacked one of the Regulators so I could get away."

"Show me," he encouraged.

She started down the passageway.

"Wait." He pulled her back, suddenly aware that something was wrong. "What aren't you telling me?"

"What do you mean?"

"Without a talisman or a guide, outsiders can't see in this world," he explained. "You should only be able to see churning mists. The vapors are a barrier, in case someone like you accidentally stumbles inside."

She pulled aside the jacket collar and he saw what he hadn't noticed before, the thin gold band that encircled her neck.

"I'm sorry," he whispered. A queasy feeling of defeat rose in his stomach. The trapper who had kidnapped him had locked a similar ring around his neck so he could see in Nefandus. The shackle had also marked him as a newly arrived *servus*. After the master had made him immortal, the fetter had been removed. Samuel could still remember the sickeningly sweet smell as the magic dissolved the metal. He didn't know how to free Maddie, and he didn't think she'd be able to cross through the portal with the binding on her neck.

"What?" she asked, but before he could speak, she answered her own question. "I'm stuck here now, aren't I? I'll be a slave like you were."

"Did you read about this place in one of your books?" he asked.

She shook her head. "Berto told me everything he could."

"We'll find a way to free you," Samuel promised, not believing his own words.

She nodded, but the color had drained from her face and he knew by the way she was chewing her lip that she didn't believe him, either. She whipped around, suddenly determined. "We'll worry about that later. Right now we need to free the others before they're executed."

He followed her, ducking below the outcroppings of black mold. The dank, musty smells became stronger as they wound deeper into the dungeon. Rusted lanterns lit their way, giving off no more than faint light, and the flickering flames made their shadows jump across the wet walls.

In a small, circular room, Maddie stopped to stare at the maze of cells and entryways. "I don't know which tunnel to take," she said. "Maybe we should go back. I think I made a wrong turn. I don't remember this place."

"It's all right." Samuel bent down, certain that if she had come through here she would have left a trail of footprints.

"What are you doing?" Maddie asked, her voice rising. "We've lost too much time already." She pushed aside a wispy spiderweb that covered an unexplored passageway and started in without him. "Maybe this one will lead us in the right direction."

And then her voice echoed happily back to him.

"There!" she yelled. "I found it."

He plunged through the gluey cobwebs and turned the corner. A sudden burst of light blinded him and before his eyes could adjust, Maddie grabbed his hand and pulled him toward the glaring sunlight shining through the opening at the other end.

Together they ran incautiously past several connecting tunnels, their shoes clacking noisily on the stone floor.

An iron grid covered the entrance to the arena. They clutched the hot bars and stared out at the white sand.

"What now?" Maddie whispered and pressed her face against the rods, trying to see above her. "It's too quiet."

"I think they're getting ready for the next game," Samuel said.

Suddenly, the audience burst into applause

and jumped to their feet, clapping as an immense Regulator entered the ring. He was at least seven feet tall and looked to weigh well over three hundred pounds. He strutted around, posturing for the audience and waving. His opalescent skin looked as if it had been burned with acid. Stiff red hair jutted from his ears, nose, and the center of his head, but no one seemed repelled by his hideous appearance. Women tossed flowers at him. The petals scattered, whirling about him.

Samuel scrutinized the medals decorating his clothes, but then he noticed something that made his heart stop. The Regulator didn't have a shadow. Samuel leaned forward. The sun was poised perfectly overhead.

"The autumnal equinox," Samuel whispered. Even though in the earth realm Los Angeles wasn't on the equator, perhaps, by some slip of space or restructuring of atoms, this part of Nefandus was. Now he understood his great-grandfather's words; the Four had to swear their allegiance to each other before this day ended.

"What now?" Maddie asked worriedly.

But before he could answer, the iron gates rattled beneath his fingers. The metal grated with an ear-piercing screech and the bars began noisily inching up.

Samuel grabbed Maddie and pulled her into a burrow as three guards marched around a corner, prodding a boy in front of them with spears. The boy tumbled into the arena.

Moving as one, the guards turned and hurried back the way they had come, dragging their iron lances behind them.

Slowly, Samuel eased out and peered through the archway. His stomach fell. "He's just a kid."

"A Son of the Dark," Maddie explained. "The others told me. That's why he's being executed."

The boy sprinted haphazardly, running from one side of the ring to the other, trying to find a way to escape. His futile attempts made the audience laugh. But then exhausted, he sat down, his gaze blank and unseeing, as if fear had overwhelmed him.

The audience's laughter quickly turned to harsh, rowdy hissing and jeering. They wanted a competition, even if it was unfair.

The Regulator stomped angrily forward and snatched the sitting boy, swinging him ferociously before slamming him against his chest. The boy tried to fade, his body flickering in and out of focus.

Samuel glanced up. Thin netting had been suspended over the amphitheater. Even if the boy had turned to shadow, he wouldn't have been able to escape through the thin threads. Samuel sensed the presence of a magic binding woven into the mesh.

"What's the Regulator doing?" Maddie asked, horrified.

Samuel turned his attention back to the arena.

Maddie let out a shriek and fell against Samuel.

The spectators howled, shouting for more, their raucous noise drowning the boy's screams.

With one last effort the boy's small fingers

raked the Regulator's cheek, but his hand sank into the creature's flesh. And then, by some vile osmosis, he was gone, absorbed into the Regulator. All that remained was a bloodstain on the green satin, and even that faded, soaking into the monster.

Samuel wondered how the audience could bear to watch such a spectacle even once. Bile rose in his throat. He closed his eyes against nausea. This was a spectator sport for the residents of Nefandus, but he had the impression it wasn't solely for their entertainment. The incredible violence was also a reminder of what could happen to any Immortal who betrayed or displeased the ones in power.

"They're so perverse." Maddie's face contorted with rage and sadness. "They make vampires look like angels."

Samuel nodded. The master had told him about the exhibitions in order to threaten him and make him obedient. Regulators consumed incorrigible *servi* and Renegades to increase their powers. But, worse, if the stories he had heard were true, the boy would continue to exist, his spirit forced to witness the Regulator's evil deeds for eternity.

Unexpectedly, trumpets blared, and a brigade of Regulators entered the arena to a loud fanfare. From the gray-green tint of their skin and the insignia tattooed on their shoulders, Samuel thought they were the Guardians, members of the highest order, all females, renowned for their ferocious fighting skills.

"There's Kyle." Maddie pointed.

In a smaller archway across from them, Kyle was one of a dozen or more *servi* being led into the ring.

The trumpets sounded loudly, and the Regulators milled about, grinning maliciously, and then slowly they began stalking their game.

"We have to do something," Maddie said anxiously.

Samuel nodded. He had to help Kyle. Maybe if he changed to shadow, he could slip into the arena, grab Kyle, and bring him back to this tunnel. Then they could escape into the maze.

He concentrated on quelling his fear so

he could transform, but before he could fade, he saw Ashley. She was no longer sitting with the master, but reclining beside a member of the Inner Circle. Samuel read the crest on his shoulder and an icy fear raced through him. Even though the man looked young, he had lived forever. He was one of the first demons created from the cosmic dust.

Ashley turned and saw Samuel. She stood and raised her hand to summon the guards.

CHAPTER TWENTY-THREE

BUT INSTEAD OF signaling the guards, Ashley lifted her other hand and stretched, arching her back seductively. Her fingers grazed the billowing purple canopy, and a wicked grin came over her lips. Clearly, she liked the attention she was creating with her provocative tease. When every male around her had stopped looking at the arena to stare at her, she laughed mischievously and sat down. The Immortal with her touched her thigh and eyed her expectantly. She turned and nuzzled against him as if no one else were present.

Samuel wondered if her distraction had been a deliberate attempt to help him? But then another thought occurred to him: if Ashley could travel into the past, then maybe she could also visit the future. Perhaps she had gone there to see what awaited him and hadn't turned him in because she had already seen his downfall.

"What are you staring at?" Maddie asked, pushing impatiently around him, and then she bristled and spoke too loudly. "Ashley's one of them. No wonder I hate her."

Samuel covered her mouth, terrified that others might hear and look over the railing.

Her eyes widened as her eyes fell on what Samuel had seen. "Sledge," she whispered frantically. "What does she want with my brother?"

"Maybe nothing more than to make Berto jealous," Samuel answered, but he was no longer sure about any of Ashley's motivations.

"Then we'll deal with her later," Maddie said as if she had suddenly become his partner. "Right now we have a more serious problem."

He looked up. Kyle was the only *servus* left in the arena. The others were gone, absorbed except for lingering stains and slimy globs dotting the sand.

Two Regulators stalked Kyle, but he stayed where he was, challenging them and waiting for their attack. When they lunged at him, he cut between them, running at top speed. He dodged around two more, who tried to tackle him and block his way.

The audience roared, applauding his bravery, but his diversion infuriated the Regulators. They joined together, beads of sweat dripping down their ghoulish faces, their flat black eyes filled with hate. Kyle darted around their attack again, but as he dashed away he didn't see the lone Regulator circling to his left. The Regulator's sinewy fingers clutched Kyle's shirt. The material ripped and Kyle spun free, but another Regulator thrust an elbow into Kyle's back and knocked him to the ground, where he lay sprawled helplessly.

Two Regulators screamed victoriously and lunged forward; then, encouraged by the crowd, they each grabbed one of Kyle's arms and began dragging him around the arena to give the audience one last look at the courageous *servus* before they devoured him.

Unthinking bravery seized Samuel. He sprinted into the stadium, his body elongating and transforming to shadow as he sped toward Kyle. His father had warned him that he was too brash and careless, but he couldn't stand by and do nothing. He twirled around Kyle, making him fade, and then stole him from the startled Regulators. He sped back in the direction he had come.

Joy exploded from the spectators as if they were about to witness an important match.

The Regulators rumbled after him, shrieking angrily, their brute yells vibrating through the coliseum.

I've got you, Kyle, Samuel said telepathically and dove toward the labyrinth of tunnels, but before he reached the archway he knew something was dreadfully wrong. He spun back inside himself and materialized. Kyle fell in front of him and groaned miserably as he took solid form again. A smaller net like the one covering the amphitheater had ensnared them.

Samuel's heart sank. Maybe this was the end Ashley had seen.

The audience stood for a better look at the imprudent young hero. Some laughed. Others made fun of his foolish bravery.

A huge hand grasped his ankle, the cold fingers crushing muscle and bone as if trying to force a scream from Samuel for the pleasure of the fans. Samuel defiantly twisted around and taunted the Regulator with his silence. The Regulator grinned cruelly, bloodlust shining in her eyes. Then, with a triumphant cry, she lifted Samuel high over her head to show off her prized trophy before she slammed Samuel against her chest and squeezed, strangling him.

The Regulator's energy vibrated through Samuel, growing stronger until it became a constant, calming hum. The soothing sound eased into his mind, tranquilizing him. The crowd's cheering became a whisper, and even his own screams seemed distant and far away.

Stinging pain covered his abdomen, as if

his skin were being peeled back. He sensed his body bleeding into the Regulator, becoming part of her essence, and yet the invitation didn't repulse him, not at all. In a dreamy way he understood the rightness of what was happening; after all, he had failed to save his family, Maddie, and his best friend Macduff, and his stupid courage had probably con-demned Kyle to horrible torture before he was finally consumed.

Samuel stopped struggling. It was what he deserved. He had disappointed everyone. Now he would be punished for his failure and spend an eternity drowning in the Guardian's dark memories.

CHAPTER TWENTY-FOUR

SOMETHING TICKLED Samuel's nose. He blinked, and within his stupor he became aware of feathers fluttering around him. He drowsily glanced up. A raven had pecked its way into the netting overhead. It squirmed through the opening and glided down, its black plumage glistening with a metallic sheen. The bird flew at Samuel and, as it passed over him, nipped his forehead with its sharp beak. The pain jolted him from his trance.

Abruptly, the fetid odor of the Regulator rushed into his lungs and made him wince. He jerked back, trying to wrestle free, but the steely arms held him. The Regulator seemed unaware that Samuel was no longer spellbound. She stood stock-still, rooted in the sand, leeching his strength, as if in some kind of trance of her own.

The bird soared up, its brassy caterwauling echoing around the stadium and creating a commotion in the crowd. Then it banked and dove, its powerful wings spread wide. Its talons gripped the Regulator's scalp, tearing skin and carrying away clumps of hair. The Regulator howled and broke out of her paralysis, her face contorted in agony. She dropped Samuel and grabbed her bleeding head.

Samuel hit the burning sand and curled into an undignified ball, clutching his stomach. His chest felt wet and slick, and stung as if his skin had been scoured away. His mind refused to let his eyes look down and examine the sticky fluid seeping through his tattered shirt. He shuddered, feeling appallingly unclean. His blood had mixed with whatever vital liquid pulsed through the Regulator.

The heavy thud of footsteps vibrated beneath him. Other Regulators were coming, their harsh breaths creating foul currents of air. He collected himself and stood, his legs stiff and unsure, then looked around for his friends.

Kyle still lay in the sand, but a Regulator was crouching over him. Samuel had to do something quickly.

The audience fell silent, eagerly anticipating what would happen next. Tension filled the arena as one by one the Regulators circled Samuel. He pinched the stone totems for the coyote and the raven, calling forth his power animals, but instead of flying to his rescue, the raven cawed and fled through the hole it had torn in the netting, abandoning Samuel.

The Regulators sensed he was unprotected now. They lumbered forward, casting sideways glances at each other as if they intended to fight over him.

His great-grandfather had warned him not to summon his guardian spirit, the mountain lion, until he had the power, but he didn't know what that meant, and he needed help now. He had no choice. His fingers closed over the stone, and he rubbed the totem.

Unexpected energy surged into his blood, spreading through his veins, pumping from his head to his toes. His limbs tingled. His temples throbbed and his tongue prickled. When he opened his mouth, canine teeth jutted ominously over his lips and a primitive growl rasped from his throat.

Astonished, he realized the mountain lion wasn't coming to his rescue; he was becoming the beast. Feverish aches rocked his body. His muscles bulged and stretched. Knees, hips, and elbows popped, then reconnected into the skeleton of a quadruped, forcing him to stoop. When his hands touched the burning sand, claws spiked from his powerful paws.

His vision changed. Everything blurred, and then, with an intensity that made his eyes sting, the world came back into sharp focus. He was keenly aware of textures, movement, and details he had never noticed before, and in that same moment, his hearing increased until his ears detected every breath and rustle of the coliseum mice.

He became the predator and sniffed the air, catching the scent of fear. He fixed his attention on the Regulator holding Kyle. Brutal energy stirred within him, and then he leaped, the power in his thighs propelling him in a graceful arc.

The Regulator screamed and fell back, hitting the sand with a loud thud. Kyle rolled to the side, his body limp, eyes half closed.

The mountain lion jumped away and skidded on his paws, then spun around, tail lashing. His claws unsheathed and he swiped the Regulator as she tried to stand. Her skin tore free and with it came the rich odor of victory. Samuel savored it, breathing the aroma through his mouth. He turned his head and roared, lord of the forest, the shriek resounding in the hot afternoon. Then, belly low to the ground, he began to hunt again, his vision pure and perfect.

Dismayed, the Regulator stood and faced the giant, stalking cat.

The audience exploded with applause and cheers, clearly thrilled that the Regulator was going to give them more blood sport.

Kyle lay disoriented and stunned, then slowly stood and limped back to the archway. The other Regulators ignored his escape. Their energies were focused on the mountain lion.

Samuel snarled, warning them away. His consciousness had melded with that of the animal, and brute instinct ruled. He sensed every move, every approach around him. Pride stormed through him and he knew he could win, but with his arrogance came the cold rush of metamorphosis. What had he done? His tail bones gathered painfully and snapped back into his spine. The lethal claws flattened, turning back into powerless, bleeding fingernails.

He willed himself to remain a mountain lion and tried to summon the primitive power of the beast. He cried out, but the clamor was a weak and defeated, all-too-human yell. He stood on two back paws, his head wobbling uncontrollably, as sleek muscle and fur turned back into teenage boy.

Three Regulators smiled mercilessly and charged, their foul stench filling his nostrils, but he didn't turn and run. He only coughed and sputtered, bewildered. He stared blankly, dull-witted. His mind hadn't yet taken over complete control from the instinctual intelligence of the beast, and he was left in a confused limbo. But just as the Regulators were set to fall upon him, they abruptly turned away and charged in different directions.

Samuel blinked, trying to see what was happening. The audience was in an uproar, laughing and screaming. He sqeezed his eyes shut, and when he opened them again, his human vision had returned. Spectators were climbing the steps toward the exits but he still didn't understand the reason for the pandemonium.

A hand clasped his shoulder and he flinched.

"Come on. We have to get out of here while the going's good." Berto pulled Samuel away and then, half yanking, half dragging him, helped him leave the arena.

"Good show," Obie said, congratulating him. "But your timing is way off. Why did you turn back before you had ripped the Regulators apart?"

"I'm not sure," Samuel said, still dazed. "What's going on?"

"The condemned *servi* are breaking free," Maddie said. "You did that."

Samuel studied the chaos in the arena. Hundreds of *servi* dashed into the ring, fading to shadow as they ran, and spinning upward in thick columns, friends holding friends, yelling and whooping as they escaped through the hole the raven had made in the magic netting.

Regulators stumbled back and forth, trying to catch the prisoners, but even though they captured some, many more escaped.

Maddie helped Samuel into a side tunnel, but her hands were unnaturally cold, and Samuel worried she might go into shock.

Kyle was waiting for them, leaning against the wall, his face pale and his eyes sunken. His shredded shirt was still saturated and dripping with something too gruesome to consider.

"Ready?" Obie asked when they were squeezed together inside the narrow passage. His finger marked the air, scribbling something unseen, and when he finished, runic letters flared, casting light across the walls and making Obie's face glow. The inscription twirled to the tunnel entrance and began closing it, stitching magic over the archway.

"Stop!" Samuel yelled and strode toward the corridor they had just left.

Obie swept his hand in a semicircle and the letters hovered, shimmering and casting off golden dust.

"You can't go back," Berto said. "We have to get out of here before the commotion dies down."

"I've got to find Macduff," Samuel explained.

Kyle stepped in front of him, blocking his way. "You said yourself he was a turncoat."

"We've all fallen for Ashley," Samuel answered calmly. "Why should Macduff be any different? He was once my closest friend. I can't leave him now."

"He's probably escaped with the others," Maddie put in.

"Maybe," Samuel said. "But I need to make sure."

Berto and Obie exchanged anxious looks.

"We'll meet you at the portal," Kyle said, but his worn expression didn't appear optimistic. "The one that leads to the fortune-teller's shop."

Obie took Maddie's arm. "I'll make sure she gets out."

"I'll be fine," Maddie answered bravely, and shook her arm free, but her fearless remark didn't hide the trembling in her fingers.

Samuel stepped around Kyle, and as he ducked under the ancient letters a whiff of burning roses settled over him, and residual magic spread through him with a gentle blessing.

Minutes later, he found Macduff cowering in a dark alcove, tears flowing down his cheeks.

"Why didn't you try to escape with the others?" Samuel asked.

"I was too scared," Macduff said and

looked away, ashamed. "Leave me. This is what I deserve."

"If you feel that way a week from now," Samuel said, helping his friend stand. "Then I'll bring you back here myself. I promise."

But as he lifted Macduff, Samuel sensed something behind him. He whirled around, and what he saw made his heart beat faster. A Regulator blocked their only exit.

CHAPTER TWENTY-FIVE

SAMUEL SLUMPED against the wall, depleted. He couldn't save his friend or himself. "I've failed again," he mumbled.

"No, you haven't," Macduff said forcefully. "There's no failure in trying."

"Right," Samuel said, unconvinced, and let out a hopeless sigh. "Every time I think I'm going to rescue you, I get you into a worse fix."

"You'll find a way out," Macduff said, wiping his face and sitting up straighter.

Samuel shook his head. "Not this time."

"I won't let you give up," Macduff said and scrambled to his feet. He let out a defiant cry, and ran at the Regulator.

"What are you doing?" Samuel yelled and shot after him. He grabbed Macduff around the waist, but Macduff spun free. "You fool, come back! She'll catch you for sure!"

At first he thought Macduff had panicked and that his reckless charge was a stupid attempt at escape, but then Macduff threw himself at the Regulator. He grabbed her neck and clung tightly. The Regulator froze, as if her instinct to absorb Macduff were stronger than her duty to stop two Renegades.

"Go," Macduff yelled through clenched teeth. "You can get away now."

"I'm not going without you." Samuel yanked Macduff's arm.

"Please," Macduff whispered, his voice growing faint as his chest melted rapidly into the Regulator. "Let me be the hero for once."

"No!" Samuel screamed. He cringed,

unable to bear the sucking sounds the Regulator made as she ingested Macduff. As he turned to run, Samuel thought he caught Macduff's soft expression staring out at him from behind the Regulator's lurid eyes. His heart shuddered and he stood, frozen. Had it only been his imagination? Then, as quickly as the illusion had appeared, it was gone.

Samuel fled through the maze of tunnels and at last burst out into the scorching sunlight. Hot wind rushed against him, drying his tears and searing his mouth and lungs. He quickened his stride across a meadow, hoping to outrun his sorrow, but his grief stayed with him.

Finally the city streets opened in front of him. He came to the crossroads where he had paused earlier that day and slowed his pace. At the end of the next alley, Obie and Berto each held one of Maddie's hands; together with Kyle they were walking toward a gray stone wall.

"Wait!" Samuel rushed toward them.

They turned, relieved to see him.

"Stop!" was all Samuel could get out.

"What's wrong?" Kyle asked, glancing at

his wristwatch. "We don't have any time left."

"The shackle on Maddie's neck," Samuel said, breathlessly. "She can't go through the portal with it on."

"That's easy to fix," Obie said confidently, and his fingers worked a spell. Words formed, wavering in the breeze, and then the incantation spun around the gold band. The shackle dropped to the ground with a loud clatter.

"Hurry!" Kyle yelled. "The portal is closing."

Obie and Berto plunged into the wall and disappeared. Maddie dove through after Kyle. The gray stones rippled around her as if she had stepped through a veil of water.

Samuel followed her. Immediately a gluey film covered him and his thudding heartbeat slowed. His body was suspended, unable to move as his molecules rearranged, configuring to the patterns of earth's realm. Then a dull ache pulsed through him. He fell forward and found himself in front of the fortune-teller's shop in Chinatown. No one seemed startled by his sudden appearance.

"I bet they found a replacement for my

part," Kyle said unhappily, as if this had been an ordinary day. He walked away and joined Obie and Berto near the bakery. They huddled together, casting backward glances at Samuel and Maddie.

"Why is he thinking about work?" Maddie asked incredulously. "*National Geographic* and the Discovery channel are going to beg for our story. We'll be rich beyond belief."

Her excitement was contagious, but Samuel knew it was unsafe for anyone in this world to learn about Nefandus.

"Let's call the *L.A. Times*," Maddie squealed, but then she scowled. "We can't do that. What am I thinking? People here would never understand the risk. Weapons and armies are no match against magic."

"You're right," Samuel agreed and tenderly drew her to him. He liked Maddie, but he could never be with someone as good as she was until he learned to control the dark instincts that lived deep within him.

"You and me," she whispered dreamily. "Maybe we can do something."

He was filthy, covered with dried blood and dirt, but she caressed the mark she'd made on his cheek with the crucifix. And then she surprised him by pressing closer and sliding her hands up his back.

"We'll make it our secret, our crusade, and find a way to save the world," she whispered.

His heartbeat quickened and he breathed deeply, trying to calm the yearnings awakening inside him. He lifted her chin, forcing her to look up at him again. She blushed shyly as he stared into her innocent eyes.

He hesitated.

"Don't you want to kiss me?" she murmured, desire making her bold.

"Of course I want to kiss you, Maddie," he whispered in a low, hoarse voice not his own. He bent closer, pulling her precariously near, sensing the danger and at the same time relishing it.

Her tongue flicked over his lips, startling him. His breath skipped. His dark side pulsed through him and he tentatively kissed her, holding back, afraid, and then at last he took in her luxuriant life force, stealing it from her. His lungs exploded with her sweetness, and he eagerly drew more.

A hand clasped his shoulder and yanked him back. He blinked and stared into Obie's sympathetic eyes.

Maddie stumbled, uncertain, then rubbed her chest as if it felt hollow.

Samuel realized what he had almost done and a sickening feeling rushed over him.

"You'll be all right," Samuel said to answer Maddie's worried look. He hadn't drawn enough life from her to do much damage. Her soul was vibrant, and he knew she would quickly replenish her lost spirit.

"We can't let you remember," Kyle said, and he gently took Maddie's hand.

She tried to pull away, but Obie quickly wrote an incantation in the air. A halo of inscriptions encircled Maddie, and a faraway look came over her.

"Sorry," Obie said to Samuel. "I had to do some quick thinking."

"What do you mean?" Samuel asked, staring

at Maddie and wishing he could truly kiss her.

Obie shrugged. "You erase one memory, you erase a lot, and adding memories is even trickier."

Berto patted Samuel's back consolingly. "She's been gone for almost six days now. Her parents are going to be upset and wonder where she's been. We had to come up with something believable."

"Believable for her anyway." Kyle smirked.

Suddenly anger burst into Maddie's eyes. She peeled off Samuel's jacket and handed it to him, fuming.

"I'm sorry," Samuel said, not sure yet why she was so angry with him or what he was apologizing for.

"I am going to be in so much trouble and for what?" she said. "You convinced me to go with you to the desert for a week to watch for aliens and flying saucers, and now you tell me you don't even believe in extraterrestrials? Just wait until I tell Sledge." But in the middle of her tirade, she stopped suddenly and touched her neck where the shackle had been, as if another memory, stronger than the ones Obie had planted in her head, had suddenly broken into her thoughts. She blinked, confused.

"What?" Samuel asked.

"Forget it," she said irritably and walked away, but at the corner she looked back as if she had reconsidered. "It was fun anyway," she shouted. "Call me when I'm off restriction!"

"I promise," Samuel yelled, but then the setting sun caught his eye. "The oath," he said, turning to face his friends. He raised his fist into the air. "I swear my allegiance to the Four."

Obie clasped his outstretched hand. "I pledge my loyalty and never-ending life to the Legend and to the Four."

"Until the downfall of Nefandus," Berto added and clenched his hand around those of the other two.

"I solemnly vow the same," said Kyle.

The Four had come together. But even though they were safe for now, Samuel understood that soon they would have to return to Nefandus and fulfill their destiny.

Don't miss the next

SONS OF THE DARK book

outcast

Kyle started back down the path, determined to confront his friends. But when he reached the last hibiscus bush, Emily blocked his way.

"Why did you ask me to meet you here if you were just going to ignore me?" she asked, challenging him. "That's so rude."

Kyle stared at her, dumbfounded. "I'm sorry," he apologized. "You must have misunderstood. I didn't ask you to meet me."

"I know what you said, " she insisted. Her face flushed with a mixture of anger and embarrassment.

"When?" he asked.

"Today!" She seemed to be trying hard not to become flustered. "In class. Did you forget?"

"That's impossible," he answered, shaking his head. "I cut biology today. To go to an audition."

Her eyes widened, and then narrowed in a glare. "Do you think this is the kind of club I would go to on my own?"

He started to say no, but she didn't give him the chance.

"Is this some kind of head game you're playing with me?"

"What?" he asked, baffled, and studied her face to see if she were teasing. "Why would I do that?"

"Other girls warned me about you. I should have listened."

He started to defend himself, then paused, considering. She seemed genuinely upset, but none of what she said made any sense. Maybe she was crushing on him and this was her weird way of letting him know she wanted to hook up. But Emily could have had anyone she wanted. So why would she have chosen him?

"Well?" she said, interrupting his thoughts.

"You didn't have to make up a whole elaborate story," he answered, grinning sheepishly.

Now she was the one that looked confused. "What do you mean?"

"If you wanted to go out with me, all you had to do was ask," he continued. "I would have said yes."

"*You* asked *me*!" she shouted. "You practically begged!"

To his astonishment, she turned and walked away. He watched her shove her way through the crowd, but before he could go after her, Berto found him.

"C'mon, we're going over to Cantor's for deli." Berto acted as if nothing were wrong, as if he hadn't just moments ago betrayed Kyle.

"I'm heading back to the loft," Kyle answered brusquely. He couldn't have it out with Berto, not here. Fights were starting to break out in front of the club, which meant the cops would be there any minute. He didn't want to spend the night in a police station.

Berto stared at him. "What gives? You sound pissed."

"Why should I be?" Kyle asked, and then something inside him let go. He needed to get away before his anger turned into blows. He stepped around Berto without saying anything more and jogged over to his rusted Chevy Impala. He started the engine. The tail pipe belched black smoke, and he slammed his foot down hard on the accelerator.

He hated the familiar emptiness in the pit of his stomach. It reminded him of his childhood, when everyone had been against him. But he wasn't helpless now, as he had been then. If his roommates wanted to get rid of him, they didn't need to spread lies about him. His life would be easier without them. He'd leave them behind and start over.

LYNNE EWING is a screenwriter who also counsels troubled teens. In addition to writing all of the Daughters of the Moon books, she is the author of the new companion series Sons of the Dark. Ms. Ewing lives in Los Angeles, California.